Freshmeat

Nyla's Dual Reality: The Freshman Year

by

RAI ADAMS

Acknowledgements

I must acknowledge the brilliance of my editor, the positive spirit of her heart and her determination to see me win. My editor Brittany N. Jones has helped me through this entire process beyond editing my book. She is a true believer and an absolute blessing.

I must acknowledge and show gratefulness to Demond Q. Johnson who was a partner in the great mastermind concept of my book cover design. I cannot show enough gratitude to him for his continued support.

A huge acknowledgment to Leah Skeete Walker, my book designer, who took my ideas and brought them to life on the book cover.

A major acknowledgement to Nikki Shedrick and Aseelah Shareef for the beach memories that will last me a lifetime. I didn't know we 'tanned' until I met them.

Dedication

Thank you to my inner and outer circle of human beings who made writing this book brilliant. My longest and faithful friend, Elliot J. Gamble, who has always believed in me and told me exactly what I needed to hear at the times when I did and often times didn't want to hear it. I can't say enough about the experiences that have brought me to this very moment, and I am now grateful for each and every one of them.

I am forever grateful for DDG! Nikki, Aseelah, and Charmane (RIP) are my best friends and my chosen sisters. I can never remember a time that they weren't in my corner during my adult life.

I do this for Beau, for my nieces and nephews, for my mother, and those who can't do it for themselves. I am a rose that grew from concrete.

The Intro

Hey out there! Please don't judge me. I'm about to share my life, heart, and soul with you. It may not all be pretty, but I'm beautifully made because of it. Oh, by the way, I'm Nyla… Nyla Howard, but my family and close friends call me Nyla Bell or just Bell. I'm quite the catch; too bad I didn't always let the best ones catch me. During my college years, I was all up and down this country and to islands nearby having a great time and looking for the next adventure while I aced my way through school. Yes ma'am! Yes sir! Nothing stopped me from getting those grades! I could not lose my scholarship and go back to the slums, the ghetto, the projects-whatever you want to call them; I could not and would not go back there. I almost came close twice, but I made it through.

We'll get to those stories later.

Right now, I want you to know from the beginning: I'm two-faced- I mean really two-faced… Now see, I know what you're thinking, tramp, liar, or worse, but Friend, didn't I ask you not to judge me? I'm gonna share some things with you. I want you to know all about me. I bet we have a lot in common...

Prologue

I thought I had done it all until *that* day in August 2001. That gorgeous summer day, the sun was coming up and sparkling outside of my window; I was enjoying the light on my skin. What a perfect way to wake up and turn over to a cute text from a man I craved all the time since Freshman Orientation over a year ago. I knew that we should just be friends, but that man's skin was caramel brown with hazel brown eyes that shined bright and hypnotized me like the sun. He was big and bold. He knew how to look at me with just the right gaze that made all my body parts pulsate every single time. Gosh, I wanted to fight it, but that gaze, my goodness that gaze, and that flawlessly gorgeous soft silky skin. He was the man of many of my dreams, wet or not. He had all the right features in all the right sizes for all the right occasions. Oh, my goodness, how I longed for that man!

The text read, *Hi Nyla. It's Jeffrey. I really want to come over to see you.* So, I called him to confirm. He said that he wanted me for breakfast, so I was more than willing to oblige him by opening my doors early for business. He came in the front door with a purpose- to make me remember him forever and ever in all ways possible.

Jeffrey ate off my plate that morning like he was starving for steak, so I made sure he had the potatoes, green beans, and dessert to go with it. He wanted breakfast, but I gave him a three-course meal. This man was my forever kryptonite. I couldn't help wanting him whenever he was around. Janet Jackson was right when she said, "Like a moth to a flame." He had me like he was on death row, and I was his last chosen meal.

What the hell was I thinking? Hell, I wasn't thinking. I was completely in the moment, loving being the owner of my very own exclusive breakfast club. This man must have been thinking about me all night long. He woke up at the crack of dawn feening for my Midas touch, and well, you know me, I gave it to him. It was Jeffrey. He needed it! He needed me. He needed his Nyla, and I enjoyed every bite and lick of his lips. He knew how to get me every time. As I drifted back off to sleep, I could only replay the thoughts of Jeffrey and breakfast in my mind, but when I woke up it started to settle in.

SHIT! I did it again! Wet bed with no Jeffrey in it. These dreams of this man seemed more and more real every single time.

Since the beginning of my college life, I have been hooked onto this man. He's never been my man, but I

6

couldn't tell my Virginia Downtown Lady Brown friend that because every time he was near her, she perked up and wanted to drop seasoning all over him. Too bad it wasn't real- yet.

Chapter 1- Am I Fresh Meat?

I met him at Freshman Roundup during our second day of orientation the summer before my freshman year. He was one of the student ambassadors, and I could not stop staring as he stood up in front of my small group and explained to us the ABCs to university life at The Florida State University. I knew that I was in a little trouble because I had a boyfriend of four years from high school back home waiting for me to return in two days, and I just could not stop staring at this sexy-smooth-silky-skin-caramel-Frappuccino. Oh Lawd! How I wanted to suck all of his whip cream. My goodness; I would want a Venti size of that right there.

"Hello Nyla. Earth to Nyla. Come in Nyla," Sharon whispered as she obviously saw me drooling over this succulent specimen in front of me.

"Huh. What? Girl what's up? I was listening because you know I am nervous about being a freshman so far away from home," I lied. I was thinking about just what she thought I was thinking about. Mr. Jeffrey had all of my attention.

"Yeah right. Okay, Nyla. Whatever you say. I see how you looking at Mr. Caramel. I know he's fine, but damn girl. Remember Rashad?"

"Stop it Sharon. You know I love me some Rashad. I was just listening attentively to help me for the fall."

"Girl, for you to be so smart, have graduated in the top ten of your class, and to be from the inner city, you can't lie worth a damn. You are absolutely drooling over that man. Trust me, I understand, but don't get sucked in so soon. Remember what I told you. Girl they are looking for *Fresh Meat*. All of these upperclassmen want our goodies. Don't hand them over- especially during orientation. Child, you'll never be able to live that shit down."

Sharon was in full big sis mode, even though she wasn't my sister and she was only about seven months older than me. That made her eighteen while I was still seventeen, but she was acting like it was seven years instead of seven months. However, she was right. I was drooling over that man, but I damn sure wasn't going to tell her! Come on Friend, I was born on one day, but it wasn't yesterday. I wasn't admitting shit, so as I continued to lie, I began to really think about my path to this point.

If anybody would have asked me if I thought I would make it this far, my answer would have always been and still is yes. I knew I was destined to be here. I knew very early that something was not right about my life, and I could not stay in a house of complete dysfunction. A house of abuse and a mother's "love," but thirst for her own needs made times unbearable for me. Hell, it made times unbearable for all of us, so there I was, a freshman in college with a full ride for being a first generation college student, for being in the top five percent of my graduating class of over five hundred students, for having over a 4.0 grade point average, and for being of a family of nine-2 parents and 7 kids, living just a split hair above the poverty line.

Nyla Howard, girl you made it, I thought. *You have arrived, so what will you do to stay here and excel past the noise of your past to the purpose and promise of your future?* Maybe one day, I'll tell you all about the thunderous noise of my childhood. My upbringing is a story about love, hate, fate, sex, drugs, and no damn rock and roll. I may share all of that with you one day, but today is not that day. Just know that I was such a good girl

9

growing up. Most people called me, "Schoolgirl" because I was always reading or studying. But, my love for school was almost equally matched with my love for boys. Though boys were a close second to school, I sometimes blurred the lines and skated on the edge of no return.

School was a great place in my life. We understood one another. I loved her, and she loved me right back. She was my best lover; too bad I wasn't into girls because we would have made an awesome couple. She "got" me. There were a couple of times when I neglected her, and I have to admit that Rashad and Jeffrey were those times- Rashad, for so many reasons and Jeffrey, for all the right reasons at what seemed to be all the wrong times.

I kept smiling about my life up to this point, and as I hugged Sharon goodbye at the end of our last day of orientation, I was a little emotional and didn't know why.

"Girl what the hell is wrong with you? Why the waterworks?" Sharon teased.

"I'm just happy- like really happy," I replied with eyes full of tears. All I kept thinking inside was, *Girl, if only you knew all I've come through, you would be crying for me too*, but who the hell is dwelling on that? I sure won't.

Friend, my life is colorful to say the least, but trust me, I'll tell you all about it eventually.

Chapter 2- Dear Mama

Well, on the plane ride home, I kept thinking about how great orientation was that weekend. "Orientation was the bomb- over the top fun," I kept telling my mother. I felt like a kid in a candy store with endless amounts of money. I could not wait to get back on campus. There are so many opportunities for me in Tallahassee, and I am going to really excel there. I talked the entire flight home. My mother listened attentively. She was excited and proud of me all at the same time.

"Nyla Bell, I am so proud of you. You made it, girl. You made it." She smiled big and tears began to rise up in her eyes.

"Mom, please don't cry, please."

It was too late. The waterworks began and she was overcome with excitement and joy. She just stared at me from her seat, 3B, with such glee.

"Mommy, thank you for being here and raising me in such a profound way. I really thank you for growing up and taking great care of us like I know you know how. I know it was not easy, but I thank you for doing all you could to get me to this point."

"Excuse me, ma'am, would you like some snacks?" the flight attendant asked me as I barely opened my eyes from my daydream. It felt good to dream of a mother that would be there for her children. It made me smile to dream of a mother that would love her children through all of their childhood accidents and experiences. It caused another tear, then another, and another as I shook my head knowing that I didn't have that type of mother. The attentive flight attendant brought me out of my pleasant daydream and back to my challenging present: I didn't have the mother of my daydreams. I had the careless and unstable mother of my reality.

I wiped the next escaping tear streaming from my face and smiled with a pleasant response, "No thank you, ma'am. I am fine; thank you."

She smiled and slipped me a few napkins. I took them politely as I returned my gaze to the nice cozy but empty 3B next to me. I shook my head hoping this would shake the tears dry in my eyes, but they kept coming.

*

I still didn't understand how a woman could have children and desert them. How could a person not love their

12

offspring enough to do whatever necessary to be strong enough to raise and care for them? Growing up, some people would say that our family looked great, and we did- on paper. The truth was that we were a mess- an absolute mess.

However, my father was to be praised for doing all of the work to raise us right. He worked full-time, cooked all of our meals, and made sure that we kept rigorous schedules in and out of school. When I got older, I realized that he wanted us to be overly active to distract us from the fact that we had an absent mother.

Let me just tell you right now, Friend. My mother isn't dead- she's just absent, an empty vessel, not worthy of the love that anyone has for her. To me, everything about her is gone. My mother, Ms. Nancy F. Howard, is an addict. I learned to say it that way in therapy sessions. After years of being heartbroken, my Dad signed us all up for counseling because my mother was a damn category twenty hurricane with catastrophic tornadoes that accompanied her.

You name it, she had been addicted to it. As I got older, I used to say that she only had the six of us because she became addicted to having children, but to me she loved nothing more than herself.

As another tear successfully escaped my eye, I felt my tears turning into anger. I felt it coming faster than I could escape it. My vision started to see the spectrum that led to destruction- yellow, orange, red, but thank goodness before I was in complete red mode, I heard my father. *Ny. Ny Bell. Baby you're okay. You're fine. Everything is okay. Breathe! Baby Bell, I need you to breathe, please. Give me your hands. Focus your mind. I love you darling, Baby. I love you. Remember, do as Dr. Newton told you.* And, so at that moment, thousands of feet high in the sky, my father brought me back to my current reality.

"I am an overcomer! I am a conqueror! I am a fighter! I am strong! I am a winner! I make my destiny, and it is great. I am marvelously made, and God loves me." As I quietly said these positive affirmations, I reached into my bag, took one of my A-pills, and refocused my heart. I switched the music playing in my ears to Babyface and Pebbles, "Love Makes Things Happen," and soon began to smile about my future life in Tallahassee.

Chapter 3- Sweet Connections

It had been a great three-day orientation, and I stayed an extra day to visit with some connections that my mentor, Yolanda, from my high school magnet program back home contacted for me while I was in Tallahassee since I was traveling there by myself. They had been very hospitable, and I appreciated all of their help and support during my time there. It was bittersweet for me because though I didn't have anyone to go with me to orientation, my mentor's contacts were right there to support me.

Mr. and Mrs. Elliott picked me up from the airport and truly opened up their home. The night before orientation, they took me to dinner and provided a car ride tour of Tallahassee.

As we took the turn from the airport down a particular street, Mr. Elliott began his touring dialogue.

"Nyla, this street turns into Monroe Street, which is one of the four major streets in Tallahassee. If you make a left there, you will run into the campus of Florida A&M University, better known as FAMU, Rattler Country. FAMU is my alma mater. Mrs. Elliott is one of your Seminole women. We met on FAMU's campus, though.

She did her studying at FSU but did all her loving at FAMU," Mr. Elliot said jokingly.

Mrs. Elliott's face turned bright beet red, but she shook her head in agreement. As we continued to drive along, I began to notice the change in buildings and landscape. As I was preparing my question, like a good tour guide, Mr. Elliott anticipated it and began to speak again.

"To your left, you have our state's capital, and if we turn right, you will be on Apalachee Parkway. Down Apalachee, you will find some of the best eating and shopping in Tallahassee. You have the Apalachee Mall, Bennigan's Restaurant, Marshalls, Smoothie King and a host of other restaurants and shops. If you keep straight down Apalachee Parkway, you'll run into Capital Circle, which is again the circle around Tallahassee. It's truly impossible to get lost in Tallahassee and inexcusable to be late anywhere because getting to anywhere in Tallahassee takes fifteen minutes or less."

As we veered onto another road, I could see the landscape changing again.

This time, Mrs. Elliott said, "Nyla now we transition from the college sides of town to the more family residential area of Killearn. Thomasville Road will lead you all the way into Georgia and has some of the most beautiful home communities in Tallahassee."

As we turned onto their street, she was telling the absolute truth. The homes in this area of town were huge, unique, and desirable. The Elliott's had a gorgeous and rather enormous home in Killearn that sat on several acres of land; it was ideal for entertaining. Their driveway was paved with small lights that led to their huge circular driveway. It was obvious that they had made a real home for their family.

They had three boys and three dogs. The story was that the boys were all really competitive and so they each had to have three of everything- including their pets.

Their home was immaculate and full of murals, portraits, and trophies of their sons. It was clear that their children were their pride and joy. As you walked through every part of their home, you saw a "Certificate for Perfect Attendance" expensively framed and awards for this Science Fair or that competition tastefully placed throughout. All over their walls, I marveled at their family vacations and yearly Christmas photo shoots. Honestly, I would have showcased these boys and men as well. They were all drop dead gorgeous. From their bold brown eyes to their fit physiques, these boys to men were eye catchers.

That wasn't the best part, though. From the pictures, their sons seemed like pretty cool and genuinely nice guys.

Their youngest son Franklin was fifteen and was out of town with his brother, Jordan, who was seventeen visiting their older brother, Elias, who was twenty and a junior at Howard University.

The Elliotts were awesome people, and I felt so good about them knowing they were in Tallahassee for me whenever I needed them. "They are such good people," is all I kept thinking as we began our descent into the Miami area.

*

As the plane landed and pulled into the gate, I turned on my phone and called Rashad. Like I knew he would be, he was already curbside waiting for me. As I waited for the airplane doors to open, I was thankful for two things. One, that I packed everything in one small carry-on bag so I could exit as soon as the doors opened, and two, that my best friend, Kendra's dad worked for Delta Airlines and got me a wonderful first-class seat for my graduation gift. Kendra's parents were like my second set of parents. Kendra was my bestie, and we'd been friends since we were five. We met at church, and one thing my Dad tried to always do was keep us in church. We didn't go to the same high school, but she knew everybody.

Therefore, I went to Tallahassee in style. I felt so important and realized that my life was going to be just as important as I felt on this airplane- first class. It was too bad that Kendra and I couldn't go to orientation together. She decided to stay home and go to that other school in Miami that I wouldn't go to if someone paid me. My family labeled me a traitor because they were loyal University of Miami fans; however, my heart had always been with the FSU Seminoles.

*

I rushed off the plane and sprinted through the concourse out into the pickup area to see my heartthrob, Rashad, as he waited outside his car for me. I leaped into his arms and planted a passionate kiss on his lips that made him as well as the bystanders surprised. It was long and juicy, and I did not care who was watching. I missed him and he didn't stop me, so it was obvious that he missed me, too. For the last four years of our lives, we had not been a part for more than two days at a time.

When we first started dating, I was not allowed to have a boyfriend, so we couldn't see each other on the weekends the first entire year of our relationship. The second year, I still couldn't date, but we were both involved in extracurricular activities that allowed us to be out of the house during the week and on the weekends. Then our relationship received the best blessing ever; his parents moved two blocks down from where we lived. The families in our neighborhood were pretty close, and everyone took pride in watching out for everyone else in the neighborhood.

It was amazing to see him more often. I would tell a little white tale and say I was going to the corner store, and then we would meet up and hang out. I don't know why I even felt the need to lie- it's not like my mother was home or coherent when she was home to care about where I was or who I was with at any given time. All I had to do was make sure my brothers and sisters stayed out of her way and didn't mess up her "fun."

Our father was the only constant that we had in our lives. He worked so hard to take care of us, and my mother worked so hard to destroy it all. She was such a selfish careless woman. I vowed never to be like that, but I still loved and feared her. She was my mother, and I had to obey her- no matter what. But that shit was hard many days.

*

Rashad and I were like a good version of Bonnie and Clyde. I was his ride or die, and he was my rock. He knew all about my family and what I did daily to survive at home and excel in school. If it wasn't for him, I don't think I would have made it through that house and out of that house on my way to FSU. I loved my man; he always made me laugh and was fine as hell. He had the chest of Zeus, the Greek God. My man was drop, stop, and roll gorgeous. He could have been the leading actor in the movie, Gladiator. I never felt ashamed of him or ashamed to be with him because if he was one of the Gladiators, I was his wife, so of course I was "Shake-Your-Head-in-Absolute-Awe" gorgeous, too.

We made such a perfect couple- him with his beautiful chocolate skin and me with my caramel tone. We made the perfect ying and yang symbol. He was 6'4 and I was a nice 5'4. I loved him being so much taller than me because I never had to worry about the height of my high heels. The higher, the better for me! Rashad had the height of a basketball player but the build of a defensive line football player. He was my taller version of Michael Vick, and everybody knew how much I loved that man. If I didn't marry Rashad, I was going to marry Mr. Fine-as-Life

Michael Vick. I wasn't ashamed to admit it. Rashad knew my plan B, so his ass knew better than to act up. Though I was in Tallahassee, I would not mind traveling to Virginia to claim my Vick prize. I knew with me going to FSU, that would be "sleeping with the enemy" since he was at VA Tech, but I didn't care. I would surely stalk Michael Vick. Rashad knew he was certainly my only and my Plan A, so he never felt threatened by anyone.

*

At our senior pep rally, I felt like a celebrity in that gym. I know we had haters and they were all drooling from both sides of their mouths because we gave it to them that day. I worked at Chase Bank in downtown Miami for my senior internship and Rashad worked at KFC in the Grove, so we combined some of our funds and bought an outfit ensemble that had all the high school tabloids screaming for more. He wore an all-white short-sleeve Banana Republic linen two-piece pants set with chocolate colored Coach Crosby Turnlock Driver loafers, and I wore my all white Ralph Lauren dress with a gorgeous off the shoulder one sleeve ruffle pattern with my diamond necklace and earring set that Kendra's parents bought me for finishing in the top five percent of my class, for successfully graduating high school with no children, for being a good influence on

Kendra, and the list went on and on. The one-carat diamond earrings and matching two-carat pendant necklace made my outfit come alive to higher heights.

While sitting to hear all the names called for the awards, I fixed my hair one last time while looking in my compact. As I stared at the sparkling diamonds shining back at me, I couldn't help but shake my head at what I had to go through to keep yet another "gift" given to me from my treacherous mother.

*

"Oh, that is a nice set Ny," my mother said with sarcasm oozing through all the pores in her body. She knew exactly what to do to deflate my excitement for anything in life.

"Thank you. The Gambles said they were really proud of me and wanted me to have a special gift that I could always remember for this glorious occasion.

"Yes, it is a glorious occasion now isn't it? My second oldest daughter graduating from high school. Woo hoo! That deserves diamonds. What the hell shall they give you when you earn your first "A" in college? A Porsche?" She chuckled as she took another gulp from her huge red cup. We all knew what that cup represented. The bigger the

23

cup the worse her attitude would be, so we all stayed clear when she had the big gulp cup.

I knew better than to say anything to her when she was like that, but I was sick and tired of her taking all good things from me, so I responded with a little sarcasm of my own.

"I don't know, mother. Maybe they will. At least, they're showing some form of excite…" Before I could get the 'ment' out, "BAM!" is all you heard as I flew back. As she struck me with all the power in her backhand, it felt like my face violently went to one side of the room while my mouth went to the other. She slapped me so hard that I hit the ground and wall simultaneously.

"Yeah, what did you say little girl? What did you say to me?" my mother belted as she proceeded to whale on me like she didn't know me at all.

"Yeah, say it again; say it again lil' bitch," she belligerently hollered. As blood began to run from my mouth, my screaming father came to my rescue. Dropping all the bags in his hands, he picked her up and carried her away from me, but not before she hit me again so hard that I flew back into the wall.

"What the hell is wrong with you?" he screamed as he carried her upstairs.

"Put me down. She is crazy if she thinks she'll disrespect me. I'll kill the lil' bitch before I let her disrespect me. I am still her mother."

The next thing I hear is my dad slamming their bedroom door.

As soon as they heard the door close, all of my siblings came running from different parts of the house to help me.

"Ny, are you okay? Here, let me help you," Josh said as Ashanti ran to the kitchen to get some ice for my busted lip.

"Oh, my goodness, Nyla. Why do you always have to say something crazy to her?" Tyler asked as he helped Joshua get me to the couch.

Like usual, they helped to clean me up and tried to make me laugh, but it was no use. I was in full waterworks mode. They all just sat around me, held me in different places, and nursed my wounds while hugging me and saying, "It's going to be okay. It's going to be okay."

*

Hearing the announcer, Mr. Anderson, call my name shook me out of my nightmare of a daydream. "And the award for Most Likely to Succeed goes to Nyla Howard!"

I walked onto the gym floor with all smiles. It felt so good to know that people saw me being successful because I knew I would be. I had to be. I couldn't be anything like Nancy Howard.

Rashad and I racked up on awards from our outfits alone. We were voted Hottest Couple, Cutest Couple, and Most Likely to Get Married and Stay Together Couple. It was evident that all the Senior Superlative Awards for couples belonged to us. Rashad just laughed as we kept accepting the awards because he could care less about any of it. He was just proud to be with the most beautiful and amazing lady on the planet, me, yours truly, Nyla Howard.

*

"So baby, when will you come and visit me in Tallahassee?" I softly asked Rashad as we sat on Miami Beach watching the waves move back and forth. After the pep rally and the rest of the end-of-the-school-year things, we just chilled together.

"I don't know baby. You know my schedule is going to be crazy with classes and work, but you know it won't be long. I promise I will make it happen," he replied gently. As he reassured me with his kisses all over my lips and neck, I felt completely confident that we would be great, and all the naysayers would become believers. We would make it work.

As he moved his hands all around my body, I certainly did not object.

I love Rashad, and we had a plan that was air tight and fireproof. He would stay and attend the University of Miami while I attended Florida State University. With hopes of becoming a doctor, he would major in Biology, and I would major in English with hopes of becoming a lawyer. Once we graduated from undergrad, we would get married the summer before we went off to California to attend medical and law school. Once we finished school, we would stay in California and begin our lucrative careers and star-studded life.

"Nyla. You know I love you, right?" He was always asking me that, and my answer was always the same.

"Baby, of course I know that."

"I really need you to know that, Ny. My love is just like the waves in the ocean. They are endless, but I do have a question for you. I don't want you to get upset, but I have been thinking about this a lot lately. We are going to be far away from each other. It is going to be much farther than we have ever been, and we will both be really busy. Have you ever thought about us having an open relationship?"

He said those last two words as if he was praying that I would not snap; he braced his body just in case I did. Well, I had to give him what he was not expecting.

"Rashad, if you think we should try being in an open relationship, then I say let's go for it. Let's try it. I don't want to hold you back, and if you want to explore other people, then let's try it. I remember we had this same conversation in the tenth grade, and I flipped on you, but I'm older now and much more mature." I spoke with confidence and conviction.

"Really Nyla. You're okay with trying it?"

Friend, now I'm going for his jugular.

"Yes, baby, I am willing to try it. You know, at orientation, there were a lot of guys there. Some reminded me of you, and some didn't, so I think it would be great for us to explore other people. I think that it allows me to be with other people and be ready for the first time we are ever together sexually, too. I think this is good," I blurted and just waited for his fucking meltdown right there on Miami Beach.

"Wait Ny. I wasn't talking about sex. I was just thinking about being able to date other people without one of us getting upset or it being considered cheating."

"Oh, okay baby. Umm, no I don't think that is what an open relationship is really. I think if we are going to do it, let's do it."

"Nyla. I can't and wouldn't be able to deal with you being with anybody else- especially before me." Rashad sounded disappointed.

"Rashad, baby why not? I would think that you wouldn't want to date other people for the sake of spending your money with nothing in return? I know you are not a virgin and maybe this will allow you to get some since I haven't given it to you yet."

"Baby. No. I'll wait for you forever and a day. I just lost mine early. You know I haven't been with anyone else. Just forget I ever brought this up. I was listening to some of my friends and thought it might be a good idea."

"Uh huh," I thought to myself. "That is what your dumb ass gets for listening to your friends."

"Whatever you want to do, Rashad. I love you, and so I'll try it if you want," I restated.

"No baby. Let's forget that I even brought it up. The thought of you being with anyone else, even on a date, is making me mad right now. No, I don't want to do that."

"Ok baby. Whatever you think is best," but I was surely thinking that I got him. That will teach his ass to ever bring up that stupid suggestion again. Rashad knew he could not stand the thought of me being with anyone else. I don't know why he even tried to suggest it.

He was completely crazy over me and had been in at least five fights since we have been in high school. A couple of them had been on school grounds. Thank God they both happened on the football field and his crazy self wasn't kicked out of school.

The worst one, though, was with his so-called best friend, Willie. I told him a long time ago that his best friend and I went to elementary and middle school together, and he had a huge crush on me all those years. He just kept saying, "No, Nyla. He is over that. You know that was just puppy love." I would always say, "Ok, Rashad; just be careful." Well, he wasn't, and they became the best of friends on and off the football field.

*

For prom, he and Willie decided that they were going to double date. I suggested that we go solo, but they had it all planned out. I begrudgingly went along with it.

Rashad and I decided to wear purple and silver to the prom. He wore a black tuxedo with a silver and purple bow tie and vest with black Converses. His dark chocolate complexion reflected boldly off the crisp white dress shirt and the perfected purple and silver blended bow tie and vest complimented his skin tone to the fifteenth power. He looked extraordinary; his sterling silver football state championship ring, enhanced with diamonds from his father, just flashed brightly on his marriage finger while his sterling silver class ring with his amethyst birthstone as the centerpiece flashed from his other hand. One of his wrists was occupied with his sliver Kenneth Cole square-framed double-linked watch while the other kept the onyx and silver blended bracelet birthday gift from me company.

Again, he looked absolutely gorgeous. His nicely low-cut fade and perfectly smooth skin made him damn near perfect. When I tell you, I was damn sure ready to give him all my good goodies that night, please believe me.

I am sure he felt the same way about me because I was dazzling from head to toe. I had my dress made by one of my mentor's clients. She was well known all around the formal gowns scene in Miami and she did not disappoint me that night at all.

My dress was a silver "Coming to America" gown without the long sleeves; it had a mini train with intricate designs and sequins. Now, I know that some of you are probably thinking that it is too much, but it really was a gorgeous age appropriate gown that I absolutely loved and

31

felt special in. The silver foundation with purple accents made my entire body glimmer, and the sheer parts were accented with beautiful classic tiny black diamond crusted stones.

Rashad actually picked me up from my mentor, Yolanda's, house because my mother had been completely out of control; earlier that week, she swore to make my prom night hell, so my father coordinated with Yolanda. It indeed was a beautiful night. My brother and partner-in-crime, Tyler, better known as Ty came over and did my makeup.

You see, Ty was a beast, an absolute goddess, when it came to makeup. He had been into makeup and making things beautiful since he was about five or so. It was hard for my dad to accept at first, but he was such a great dad that he loved us all the way we needed to be loved the most. Our dad had a sense, like mothers had, to make us all believe, know, and feel that we were special. So, Ty doing my makeup was just the perfect touch needed to make me the perfect version of a royal princess that anyone had ever seen.

*

I remember Rashad ringing the doorbell and hearing everyone drill him as they opened the door. When Ty came upstairs and led me down, it was like I was walking down the aisle at my wedding. Once I was halfway down the stairs, I saw Rashad. It was magic. He must have seen me from the beginning because he had tears that flooded his eyes and a smile on his face that made me happy. His expressions made me even happier, and I strutted down those stairs with my diamond studded crystal stilettos leading the way. It was amazing, and my hair with diamond accessories made it no easier for all onlookers to drool over the entire presentation.

Friend, I looked amazing and I would have given him all of me that night if it had not been for Willie.

*

When Rashad and I walked out the door to the stretched Escalade waiting for us, I felt confident, sexy, and cool. When Rashad opened the door for me, it was revealed in a major way. Willie and his date, Jojo, both sat there with their mouths wide opened in awe, so you know me. I simply spoke in excitement for the night.

"What's up y'all! Let's get this party started!"

Willie bounced out of his daze quickly and replied, "Yes! Let get this party started!"

He made sure the driver's window was closed and pulled out his bottle of Hennessey that Rashad was ready for immediately.

"Yes!" Rashad screamed in delight. "Let me hit that."

Before I knew it, Rashad and Willie were passing the liter Hennessy bottle back and forth. It was no time until they were feeling good.

We pulled up at the Omni Hotel off of Biscayne Boulevard and stepped out of the stretched Escalade in style. Rashad held out his hand for me to step out in class while Willie just stared and let his date get out alone.

Once we made our way into the Omni ballroom, both Rashad and Willie were ninety-percent wasted. I suggested that they both get hydrated while JoJo and I danced. They both agreed, and Jojo and I ran to the dance floor for local celebrity JT Money's "Hoe Problems Ain't No Problems." This song always got everybody on the floor and dancing. It was our prom, and so we were happy that our school administration allowed our music to play. Of course, they censored all explicit language, but we didn't care. We knew all the words, so it was like our DJs were in a cappella style.

34

The DJ did not let us get a rest. It was hit after hit. All the girls were up on the floor with Destiny's Child, "Bug A Boo," then "Bills, Bills, Bills," then the DJ hit us with "No Scrubs" by TLC, on to OutKast, "So Fresh and So Clean" followed by "Sorry Ms. Jackson." We just danced on and on. By the middle of the night, most of us had our heels off and were breaking a sweat. We stopped for a little while to eat, but we made it quick and got right back on the floor. Trick Daddy and Trina's "Uh-Huh-Ok-Wats-Up-Shut-Up" had us back up and on our feet, then Mystical's "Shake It Fast, Watch Yourself" had us going. It was all about the bootie on that song!

It was too bad that Rashad wasn't quite ready to dance yet. He was still hydrating himself in the corner. Willie was up dancing with Jojo, and she was definitely shaking it fast and all over him. I took this time to dance with some of my girls in our own circle. We laughed and danced and showed how fast we could shake it, too. I didn't like dancing on guys, so Rashad knew he didn't have to worry about me taking on another dance partner. Then they played one of my songs, and I always had the center of our circle with that song, "Nasty Girls" by Vanity 6.

That was my jam, and everybody knew it- including Willie. He actually stopped dancing with his date to come over and watch. I was thinking if Rashad ever did something like that to me, we would have a problem. I didn't care though. I just danced and sang every word to that song. It was a song that made me feel sexy. I was probably about seven when I heard this song for the first time. It was one of my mother's favorite songs, too. I can remember watching her dance around the house to it and laughing as she saw me trying to mimic her. That was one of a very few happy memories I have of that woman, but that didn't stop me from loving this song. I knew all the dance moves from the video, so when the intro started everybody knew to assume the position.

"Y'all, here we go! That's my jam!" I screamed, and the show began.

That's right; pleased to meet you. Still don't wanna tell you my name. Don't you believe in mystery? Don't you wanna play my game? I'm lookin' for a man to love me. Like I never been loved before. I'm lookin' for a man that'll do it anywhere. Even on a limousine floor 'cause."

I sang those words and stared in Rashad's direction. He loved to see me put on my Nasty Girl Show. My dress was the right fit and style to show all my curves. I would lick my lips and gyrate to the bass in the song. It was funny to some of my friends because they all knew I was still a virgin and wasn't planning on having sex until marriage or close to it. I didn't care because I still danced and sang. The way I was feeling I might give it to him tonight, and so I sang.

Tonight I'm livin' in a fantasy. My own little nasty world. Tonight, don't you wanna come with me? Do you think I'm a nasty girl?

As the song faded out, all observers clapped. I laughed and bowed. It was always a show worth watching. I would be in my complete Vanity mode, so I bowed and waved as if I was in a parade.

"Girl, you're crazy, Nyla!" Kendra screamed as we walked back to our table laughing.

Although we didn't go the same high school, she knew *everybody*. It wasn't a surprise when she told me one of Rashad's football teammates asked her to go to the prom with him.

"Girl, Kendra you know I have to give the people what they want!" We laughed and slapped hands in the air as we headed back to the table.

Then the DJ hit us with Montel Jordan's "Get It On Tonite," which transitioned us back on the dance floor. That song was a good step into the slow jams that followed. One of my favorite songs, "Incomplete" by Dru Hill's

37

Sisqo, started, and Rashad made his way to me. By this time, he had sobered up and was able to stand up right to actually dance, and so we did.

Once we were together on that dance floor, it was like nobody else mattered. We were in our own world.

"Hey Rashad. Rashad man let's go. This girl trippin'!" Willie hissed as he tapped Rashad on his shoulder.

"Willie, man. I'm with Nyla. Chill. We'll be leaving in a little bit."

"Man forget this. I'm ready to go. Jojo act like she doesn't want me touching her now. Man let's go!"

Rashad said it again and this time a little more forcefully.

"Willie. Man. I'm with my girl. We'll be out in a minute. Go chill. You obviously had some more to drink. Man go sit it out."

Before you knew it, Willie said, "Man fuck you. You always up her ass," but before the last "s" could come out of his mouth, Rashad clocked him right in those foul lips. Then it was on. Willie tried to return a blow but missed. Rashad was all over him. With a combo to his face and chest, I swear his body was like a rag doll being swayed back and forth by the blows. Then it was so damn funny but sad at the same time. Rashad slapped the shit out of

38

Willie, and heaved, "Don't you ever disrespect my girl again!"

Though the show seemed like it was a five-minute battle, it lasted all of 60 seconds before the football team swarmed in and broke it up. They escorted Rashad out quickly before Administration knew what was going on. They led Willie to the bathroom.

I just remember standing there like, *Okay, I am definitely not jumping in this*. I headed towards the exit and Kendra was right next to me. Jojo actually came with us as well. Once outside, we got the background information.

"Nyla. His ass couldn't keep his eyes off you."

Now Jojo and I weren't friends, but we were cordial enough in school. She had her crew and I had mine, but we didn't have any beef.

"Then that fool wants to try and feel all over me on the dance floor while staring at you. Girl I was done with his stupid ass."

"Child, I don't know what his problem is. He shouldn't be drinking if he can't handle his liquor," I added.

"Child he wasn't drunk," Jojo said, but when we got to Rashad, we cut our conversation short.

I wanted to calm him down. Thank God it didn't take much, and our night wasn't totally ruined. We all ended up going to the TGIFriday's on South Beach and walking around until the wee hours of the morning. Unfortunately, there was no loss of virginity that night.

*

Rashad and I reminisced and chuckled about that night while we sat on the beach talking about our future together and how everything was going to work out perfectly for us.

I pleaded, "Baby you know you can't keep having a temper like that about me. You're eighteen now and there are serious consequences, babe, like jail time."

"I know Nyla. That's why I know it is good for us to be at separate schools right now, but I am going to miss you like crazy."

"I'm going to miss you, too. I just hope you don't go crazy with this distance."

"I won't, but Nyla. You're the love of my life. I would marry you right now if I didn't think your father would kill me."

"Rashad! You are crazy and right. My Dad would kill you, so we'll have to wait on that," I laughed.

"Yes, we will, but just know that I am serious about you and only you." He said with what might have been tears in his eyes, but I couldn't confirm because he looked away.

We spent the rest of the night cuddling under the stars and watching the waves come in and out. It was the perfect way to end the evening. Rashad always made me feel special, and so it was so hard to say goodbye to him, but we promised to be faithful and true to one another. I felt confident that we would be just fine.

Chapter 4- Campus Vibes

As I walked through the Union on my way to class, all I could hear was:

"Welcome to FSU! Would you like a free t-shirt?"

"Hi! Welcome to FSU. Would you like to hear about our specials?"

"Hi! Welcome to FSU. Do you know Jesus?"

Every inch of the Union was packed and covered with people sharing information about campus, or Tallahassee, or yes, even Jesus. It was unbelievable. It was like an outdoor festival in the middle of a college campus. "How cool is that?" I thought.

And the same way that there were questions being thrown from every side of the Union pathway, there were a plethora of student responses that went anywhere from pleasant to stealth mode silent.

"Not right now, I'll be back after class," one would say.

"Yes, sure!" another would exclaim.

"Yes, I know Jesus," many would even say.

Many kept walking so swiftly that all you felt was
the breeze as they zoomed by.

I was intrigued, but knew I couldn't be late on the first week of class, so I was definitely a "Not right now, but I'll be back."

It never failed though! Every day for the first week, the Union was packed. Every inch of the union was full of vendors selling things or credit card companies giving out things to get you to sign your credit away. Boy, oh boy, did so many of us fall victim to that.

There were people performing popular songs as well as others performing their original songs on the steps of Union auditorium entrance. Some days that week, especially on Wednesday, there were DJs set up playing the latest music. Even some of the FSU football players were chilling at tables in the Union.

To walk past their section was like walking past a billboard of America's Finest Athletes. They were all fine as hell. I mean light skin fineness to dark skin fineness to vanilla skin fineness. They provided all the eye candy a girl could ever ask for in the world, but I knew to keep it moving quickly. Our school was not only known for being one of the best in the state academically; we were also one of the best in football. Our record this year was predicted to be even better than last year, and I know we went all the way to the National Championship last year. We beat Virginia Tech, so this year we were living high. These dudes deserved to have everybody all over them, but I couldn't be one of them. I always had my eyes on my prize- Jeffrey. He was my ball player, Orientation Leader, everything...

"Hello." I heard coming from the table of fineness, but I dared not respond.

"Excuse me, excuse me," I kept hearing as I discreetly picked up my pace and walked swiftly by their table.

"Can I talk to you for a minute? Can you slow down? I just want to talk to you," reassured one of the fine football players.

Oh, Lord he was next to me. This succulent less than 7% body fat, 6 foot tall, light skin, perfect white teeth, clean cut, bold brown eyes, smooth soft clear skin, smelling like Polo Sports original scent man was right next to me. I could see him in my peripheral and knew exactly who he was… *Oh no! Oh no!* I thought. Walk faster Nyla. Walk faster.

"No, sorry. I can't talk. I have to get to class."

Friend, I felt like Nettie on the Color Purple when Mister was trying to get her to stop on her way to school. He twirled her around and all she kept saying was, "I gotta go to school! I gotta go to school!" I felt Nettie's pain but in a different way. This beautiful succulent man that was trying to get my attention was from the same city I was from and though I didn't know him personally. I knew that he was finer than life and I had a man, so, hell yes, I had to move fast. Not to mention, I heard so many stories about football players, especially that one, and I did not want to get caught up in all that fineness and forget why I came to school. Heck no!

But with his next excuse me, I had to reply.

"No, I'm sorry that you cannot talk to me for a minute. I must get to class," I said as I almost started running away.

"Nyla you're a damn fool. I would have talked to that fine ass specimen of a man. Did you see the arms on that brutha?" The voice seemed so real that I had to look around, but there was no one there. It was my crazy inside voice slapping me around for not talking to Mr. FSU Fine.

I told her to shut up and kept heading to class.

Once I entered into my Pre-Calculus Recitation class, I smiled in relief.

Finally, I was able to enter one class with less than one hundred people. I had been on campus for two days now, and every class had over one hundred students! I could not imagine how I was going to be able to make connections with anybody including the instructor, but I was determined to do so.

Of course, I would come back to the Union after my class and every class, for that matter, for that entire week. The Union was so addicting. It just pulled you in with all the different people you would see and all the food you could eat at the Food Court. You could literally hang out there all day and not get bored.

As I walked towards the food court, I was star struck. I mean that's when I saw them. Oh! It was like love at first sight, and there were so many of them and so many to love. They were dressed in all shades of Crimson and Cream. Some had on heels while others wore combat boots. All of them were dressed to kill. Oh, the ladies of Delta Sigma Theta Sorority Incorporated!

My mentor, Yolanda, told me that I had to always address them like that if I wasn't one. That is where I heard about fraternities and sororities, from my mentor in high school, but to see them on campus and in action was so electrifying. I knew I wanted to be a Delta from the first time I met my mentor in high school because she was so powerful and beautiful and poised. She always commanded the room with her presence, so to see these women in action on campus was like no other.

They had a table set up in the Union welcoming students, but you could tell that they were about business. They were all beautiful and alluring; their strong presence is what drew me to them. But, I was so nervous to walk past them on that first Wednesday in the Union and for many more Wednesdays. I would just walk by and stare. They probably thought I was crazy, but I was okay with that, too.

*

The Union was a great place to be in general, but Wednesdays were the best because one could actually see the real diversity on FSU's campus. There were different student organizations from the Black Student Union to SISTUHS- from the Positive Women's Coalition to Progressive Black Men, and from the Seminole Torchbearers to the Lady Spear Hunters. Also, the entire NPHC was represented from Omega Psi Phi to Alpha Phi Alpha to Kappa Alpha Psi and Phi Beta Sigma as well as the women of Delta Sigma Theta and Alpha Kappa Alpha to Zeta Phi Beta and Sigma Gamma Rho. It was obvious who liked who and who just tolerated the other as well as who did not like each other at all. There were local vendors that would be present to sell all types of natural body oils and incense and gorgeous jewelry pieces as well. I was just in love with being a college student- especially on Wednesdays in the Union. I felt like I belonged on campus, and it was amazing.

That first week of school went by like a breeze; it was such a blast. I was so excited to be on campus. I enjoyed getting into the swing of being an adult student away from home and on my own. Based on the hell that I endured at home, this felt surreal. And, I surely thank God for it.

Chapter 5- Family Matters

"Hi, Nyla Bell," sang my dad from the phone.

"Hi, Daddy," I eagerly spoke and smiled big. I loved it when he called me Nyla Bell.

"How are you darling? How was your first week of school?" he asked, concerned.

I started talking non-stop.

"I'm great, and school is amazing. I am having so much fun, and all of my classes seem pretty easy. I know I shouldn't sound so confident, but I'm taking English Comp II, Pre-Calculus, Aerobics I, American Government, Biology I, Biology I Lab, and Theatre. My professors seem to be okay for the most part, and I don't have all huge classes. My Biology lecture class is in this huge performing arts auditorium, so he wouldn't know if I was coming or going, but there are notes that we can get, and so I am still going to go to class. But, I definitely will be studying those notes. I started my campus job this week too, and it is nice. Dean Chen is a really nice man, and he is making me feel very welcome. I am excited about my Political Science class, too."

"That's cool, Ny. You still want to be a lawyer?"

"Absolutely! Dad, remember when I was in the third grade and we would watch Matlock reruns?"

"Yes, baby, I definitely remember."

"I would always say, 'Dad I want to be a lawyer just like Matlock.' You would always ask me why and I always said, 'Because Dad, Matlock is a winner. He never loses his cases.'"

"Yes, Nyla Bell, and you've been sure about what you wanted to do ever since."

"Thank you for always supporting me with your words and actions. You always say, 'Ny you can do it. I know you'll be great, and I believed and still do believe you.' I love you and I am doing my thing up here, Dad."

"Great baby. It sounds like you are figuring things out."

"Yes sir, I am and how are things there with everybody?"

"Well honey, we are all moving right along."

"What does that mean?" I said with some concern in my voice.

"Well, you know things have been trying for all of us. We have had quite a bit of tragedy to hit us."

"Yes. Please don't remind me."

"I know that you are going to do an amazing job there at FSU. I know that I can count on you to follow your own path...honey... I hate to have to tell you this…" His voice trailed off.

"What Daddy? What is wrong?"

"Your brothers got into a little trouble and are in jail."

"Umm. Wait. What type of trouble?" I asked curiously.

"Some boys were really messing with Tyler at school, so Josh, Matthew and Zack decided to do something about it. You know how Tyler is; he didn't want any trouble, but your brothers were tired of it. A couple weeks ago, Tyler came home with barely any clothes on, and a few days ago they beat the crap out of him, so your brothers went to where the boys hang out and beat the hell out of them."

"Good! That's what they get for messing with Ty. Why would anyone want to mess with him? He's the nicest one out of all of us," I said puzzled.

"Well, Ny. You know some people are not going to even try to understand him."

"I don't care if they don't understand him. He has a right to be who he is and live without stupid people messing with him."

"Well, darling that's how we all feel, but your brothers went there, a fight broke out, and one of the four boys fell and hit his head. He is now in critical condition and since Josh and Matt are of age, they've been arrested and Zack has been taken to juvenile jail.

"What! Oh no Daddy! Oh my goodness. No.

"Well where is mom?"

"Honestly, sweetheart, I don't know."

"Figures."

"Nyla. She's still your mother."

"Unfortunately."

"Come on sweetheart. Let's focus on your brothers not her."

"It's kind of hard to do that when she always seems to be messing things up. Did you look in the usual places?"

"Actually, Ny, no I didn't. I can't keep doing that. She's been gone for about three weeks this time, and I can't keep pausing everybody's life, so I decided to keep moving. You all deserve to have at least one of us that are fully committed to you.

"Daddy, you have always been committed to us and her for that matter. It is too bad she's never been committed to anyone but her damn self."

"Nyla Howard. He said in a stern voice. Watch your mouth and your tone baby please. I know this is hard but you've got to remain strong and respectful."

"Yes sir. So what is going to happen with my brothers?"

"This all just happened a couple days ago, so Matt is out on bail, but Josh's bail was denied because of his priors and Zack was release to me because he's a minor. They're both on house arrest until the proceedings in a couple of weeks."

"This is so messed up. Where are they now?

"Upstairs. Of course, they didn't want me to call and worry you, but I thought you should know baby."

"May I talk to them please?"

"Yes Ny. Hold on."

Oh my goodness. I can't believe this is happening. I'm so glad this is the weekend. How in the world would I concentrate with this happening? This is some crazy mess, and after two more hours of talking to my brothers, I got the entire story. It was a fucking mess to say the least, and poor Ty felt completely responsible.

"Ny. I promise. I never meant for any of this to happen. I can't wait to graduate and move to New York where I can be me and free." I could feel his pain and his tears as they rolled down his cheeks and through the phone to touch me and make me cry with him.

He said, "Everybody knows how much I love fashion, and so when the Administration gave us permission to have the fashion show, I was so excited. I thought everybody was cool with me. If I would have known that they were going to hate me after that show, I would have never been a part of it."

"I know Ty. I know," I assured him as he kept on talking.

"I agreed to do everyone's make up for the talent show, but when they asked me to be a model too I said no."

"Nyla, you know I was not about to model men's clothes. When I do my own shows I can be free there."

"I don't blame you, Ty. I would have said, "no," too, if I was you."

"But guess what Ny. They wanted me to dress the way I wanted to."

"What!" I almost screamed loud.

"Yes, Sis. I was surprised, too. The president of the Fashion Club asked the principal and she actually agreed to let us do it."

"Wow Ty. You must have felt good about that."

"I really did and the show was great, but what happened afterwards was horrible."

"I know. That's awful."

"Yeah. The guys didn't know it was me, but once they discovered it was me, they flipped."

"Sissie, it was awful."

Ty hadn't called me Sissie since he was a little boy, so I knew he was really hurting.

"That night and every day after, I have been their target," he said as he cried, and this time neither one of us could stop crying. All I could mutter out was, "Ty this wasn't your fault."

Friend, it wasn't his fault, and he couldn't help who he was or chose to be, and whoever wanted to judge him should look in the mirror at his own crap first. Ty was my closest brother. Even though Matt and I were Irish twins born ten months apart, Ty and I were closer. He was one of my best friends.

It was all too much for me to think about and after hanging up with them, I called Rashad to tell him about it, but he wasn't in his room or answering his cell. I just left him a few messages, took a shower, lay in bed and cried myself to sleep. Prayerfully, I will wake up and it will all be over.

Chapter 6- *Interesting* Information

The next few weeks flew by, and the ordeal with my brothers was still not settled and Josh was still in jail. Rashad and I had barely talked since I arrived in Tallahassee, but I knew he was busy and so was I, so I didn't sweat it. We were solid, so I knew we would settle in and be right back talking all the time like usual.

It was truly a gorgeous fall day in Tallahassee, and I needed to enjoy something pretty considering everything going on, so I decided to walk to work. That was truly a great idea, my spirits were lifted by the time I arrived. After about twenty minutes of being there, my boss walked in.

"Good morning Dean Chen. How are you today?" He just smiled and nodded then asked me how I was enjoying the job.

"I'm great; thank you for asking." I love working here in the College of Arts and Sciences. You are a really pleasant man to work for and I thank you for this opportunity. I promise I won't let you down. I finished the report you requested last Friday. It's on your desk along with a Future Projections report.

He smiled and said, "Thank you."

I could tell he was impressed because though pleasant, he never gave a real smile. It was always more of a grin on the face of a man in pain.

Then it happened the moment that I had dreaded and was hoping for all at the same time. Mr. Caramel Frappuccino walked through the door. Dammit! I screamed inside so loud that I thought it actually came out of my mouth. He looked so good and smelled even better. What the hell is he doing here? He is an Electrical Engineering major, and that was in the College of Engineering building.

Over the summer, I was so ecstatic when Sharon called me to talk dorm room decor but then brought him up.

"Girl you know Mr. Caramel is an electrical engineering major. His ass is smart and fine as hell. I say future hubby material."

"For who, Sharon? You?"

"No, heffa, for you. I saw how you were staring at him during small group. Jeffrey Oshea Donovan blew your breath away girl. Don't deny it."

"First of all, how do you know the man's entire name? AND Oh heck yes I am going to deny it. I love Rashad, and he's *my* hubby material."

"Child, bye! I'll let you believe that for a little while longer. Talk to you later."

Ugh! I hated her sometimes. We just met the first day of orientation, and she already knew me so well. It made me sick how she could read me without me saying a word.

After we hung up, though, I was so relieved to know that his major was Electrical Engineering and his classes were on the other side of campus because that meant the only man that made me feel different from the way Rashad made me feel was at a safe distance from me on campus. He had been the topic of too many of my conversations with Sharon lately, so I knew keeping a safe distance was crucial to my faithfulness and commitment to Rashad.

"Good morning, Dean Chen. Good morning, Nyla." His voice brought me back to the first time I laid eyes on him. As he shook Dean Chen's hand, I just sat there at my student assistant receptionist desk like a statue modeling nude for a class of freshman artists. Finally, I slapped myself inside and spoke, "Good morning, Caramel…Jeffrey. How may I assist you this morning? Do you have a meeting with Dean Chen this morning? I did not see you on his calendar."

Dean Chen interjected, "No, I believe I have a meeting with the university student ambassadors next Monday."

"Yes sir, Dean Chen. You are correct. We don't meet until next Monday. I actually came to check on Nyla. One of our responsibilities as Student Ambassadors is to check on our Orientation Small Group Students," he said as he struck me with another alluring smile that complimented the deep dimples that he had in both cheeks.

Oh Lord, I thought to myself. This man had dimples like LL Cool J, and everybody knows the ladies Love Cool J!

Dean Chen smiled, "Oh that's wonderful, Jeffrey. In that case, I will be in my office getting some work done. See you next week Jeffrey."

"Yes sir, Dean Chen, have a great day."

He immediately turned to face me, and I was so glad that I was still sitting down because I would have melted at his gaze. Just would've slithered like liquid and melted.

"So, how are you Nyla?"

"I am excellent, Jeffrey. Thank you for checking on me. That is such a nice way to make new students feel welcomed."

"You're more than welcome, Nyla." He smiled as I smiled, and we stayed that way for what felt like twenty years together. The phone rang and it broke our gaze. It was Kendra.

"Hi, Nyla. What's up? Are you busy right now?"

"Yes I am, but I can call you back in a few minutes."

"Okay, please call me back. It is important."

"Wait Kendra. Is everything okay?"

"Not really, but if you're busy, especially if people are around, call me back when you're alone."

"Umm okay, Ken I will."

"Is everything okay?" Jeffrey asked with concern in his voice.

"Yes it is, but I need to return some phone calls and get to work on Dean Chen's reports. Thank you for stopping by to check on me. See you next week."

"You're welcome, but I hope to see you before then."

"Umm okay."

"Yes, I wanted to ask you to lunch. You know, as a welcome to Tallahassee and the wonderful world of FSU. You've been here for almost three months now and so I want to make sure that if you have any questions, I can answer them for you."

"Jeffrey, thank you for the invitation, but I don't think that would be a good idea. Though I appreciate you doing your mid-semester check up on me, I have a boyfriend and I wouldn't feel comfortable with us going to lunch together."

The thoughts that I was thinking would leave me at the altar asking for forgiveness. *Lord, please forgive me for the things I want to do to this man and want him to do to me. I can only say that the flesh is weak Jesus, and mine is so weak for Jeffrey Donovan. Please help me to resist the urge to take ALL his clothes off right now. Amen.*

"Okay, I understand, but if you need anything, I am here to help as your Student Ambassador." He smiled again and just stared at me as if he really didn't want to leave.

"Thank you Jeffrey and enjoy your weekend." I smiled back not hiding my thoughts inside. I could tell that made him confident enough to leave. *Oh my goodness, Lord. I'm in trouble!*

As he walked out, all I could think was how fine that man was…there ought to be a law. *Redirect yourself Nyla…redirect girl.*

"Nyla." Dean Chen's voice brought me out of my trance. "I'm headed to my 10:00 meeting with the President and then lunch. I will see you later this afternoon."

"Enjoy your meeting, sir." Perfect time to call Kendra back. She sounded weird.

"Hey!" She picked up on the first ring.

"Can you talk?"

"Yes, Dean Chen just left for a meeting and everyone else is at a retreat, so I'm alone. What's up?"

"Well, I have something to tell you. Are you okay to talk?"

"Child, yea. Why you keep asking me that? What's up?"

"I was talking to my friend Shany today, and I was bragging about how much fun we had when we took you to Tallahassee to check into Salley Hall and how you are the only one with a damn near perfect relationship and girl, I was just going on and on and on. When I said Rashad's name, she stopped me."

"Oh? Okay. Why did she stop? What did she say?"

"She said, 'Wait- Rashad, Rashad who? What school does he attend?'" 'He's here with me at UM,' I told her, and her mouth dropped. Girl I thought she was going into shock."

"Okay Kendra! I'm dying over here. Spit it out, please."

"Well, okay, so Shany said that your Rashad is messing with her home girl, Wanda."

"Kendra, what the freak do you mean *messing with*?"

"Nyla, please don't please. You're at work."

"Please don't, please don't, please don't what?"

"She said they're together."

"What? Together? Together like what? Ok Kendra you're not giving me much. I need details. Oh my goodness Rashad. OH MY GOODNESS Rashad! This piece of crap! Oh, this mutha-plucker!"

"Breathe, Nyla. Please, Nyla. Calm down."

"Um, Kendra give me her number."

"Who?"

"You know who I am talking about! Shany. Give me Shany's number. I need to talk to her right now."

"Okay, Nyla. She's right here with me."

This is a joke, I kept thinking. *Kendra is trying to punk me.*

"Okay, Kendra let me talk to her. I want to speak to Shany and get the story from her. This muthafucker. This muthafucker. Damn him!" *There goes my two months of no cursing down the fucking drain.* "Oh my gosh this MUTHAFUCKER!" I just keep saying, screaming, whispering, and thinking over and over again.

After another hour of info gathering, I find out from Shany that Wanda and Rashad have been together for the last four months. That is around orientation, which means this bastard met her at orientation. He went to one of the first orientation sessions in the summer because he had to travel around the country for his summer job. Shany said that they just see each other at night.

63

Bottom level, Bitch, I thought. *He won't even take your ass out in public during the daytime. What type of woman is okay with that behavior? Desperate hoe!*

Shany continued to tell me how her tramp of a friend was really starting to like my man and how she wanted them to really be together.

Of course that bitch was starting to like him. Why wouldn't she? He's handsome, 300 fine, and well dressed- all of which I contributed to. That piece of shit. He must be out of his simple ass mind. Wanda sounds like a two-dollar hoe groupie with low self-esteem and a bad-fucking weave. Okay- I'm not just being mean. I saw a picture! She does have a messed up weave.

As soon as I hung up the phone with Kendra and Shany, I started crying. I mean sob in my chair crying. Thank God no one was in the office at the time. As soon as I thought I was okay, the phone rings. Thank God for caller id because I could see that it was Rashad, so I didn't answer the phone. Oh hell no! I don't and won't talk to him. I have much more in store for him. He really 'tried' the wrong girl: no fuck that! He tried the wrong bitch from Miami! I am going to deal with his punk ass city style. I began to sob again.

*

As the other set of wheels began to roll in my head, Dean Chen walked back in from his meetings. Thank God he did because I was about to destroy the office. I could not calm down. I couldn't think of anything Dr. Newton used to tell me to do. All the techniques from my old therapist went out the window right along with Rashad and my future together so thank God for Dean Chen walking in when he did. As he came through the doors, I instinctively looked at the clock and realized it had been well over two hours that I was on the phone with Kendra. That bastard Rashad.

"Good afternoon, Dean. I thought you were gone for the day?"

Just as I reached my car, I realized I forgot something. I'm glad I came back though because in one of my meetings we discussed the specifics of the Spring Family Weekend, and I wanted to ask you to be one of my Student Ambassadors for the weekend. You would be a part of my Annual Meet and Greet Barbecue. There are other functions that I would like for you to be a part of to assist in recruiting students such as yourself. I think you would be great because you are a first generation student with strong support from your family. I believe it would be great for other students to see this type of relationship. Your family would be welcomed to stay in one of our properties in Killearn. It is big enough for all of your siblings and parents. What do you think?"

"Oh, Dean Chen! This is such as wonderful opportunity. Thank you for considering me, and I know my family would be honored to be a part of such an affair." I smiled big as I lied through my teeth.

"Okay, Nyla. Since the event is not until next semester, let's get together and discuss details towards the end of this semester."

"Yes sir; that sounds great."

As he went into his office to retrieve the items he left behind, I began to sweat profusely. *Dear Lord, please let this man leave soon before he sees me have a full-fledged panic attack. I mean a real serious Nyla meltdown. What the hell was I going to do? Surely, I couldn't tell him the truth. My entire college reputation would be ruined. Yes, I'm a first generation college student, but I was never ready to tell anyone the truth about my family dynamics. Hell no! I did not need the pity parties, the counseling suggestions, or the empty promises to pray for my family and me. Fuck all of that. I would get out of this. I just needed to think it through. It's an act of kindness from above that it isn't until next semester. Plenty of time to think of an exit strategy.*

Dean Chen interrupted my calculating thoughts with his exiting salutations.

"See you next week, Nyla. Enjoy your weekend."

"Thank you, Dean Chen. You have fun with your family. I hope you can get some rest."

He smiled as if to say, 'Yeah right there will be no rest for the weary.'

I chuckled slightly at his facial expression as he closed the door.

My anxious thoughts almost immediately took over. *Oh my goodness. What the hell am I going to do?*

Chapter 7-Sleepless Night

I didn't sleep a wink last night. Just tossed and turned between so many thoughts... Rashad's cheating ass, the Dean's consideration and invitation for Family Weekend, my crazy family, and that beautiful Jeffrey, then back to my family all over again. What the hell was I going to do? The Dean was not ready for my family. Honestly, I wasn't ready for my family. I did not want them here.

When I left Miami, I left with the intentions of never going back.

I worked my ass off to get out of there. My mother, Nancy F. Howard wasn't a model citizen or mother. If I wasn't afraid of her stabbing me, I would call her Nancy. Shit she doesn't act like a mother or friend. I hadn't heard from her since I left for Tallahassee. What mother doesn't check on their child while she's away from home in college? She was no fucking mother. In the fifth grade, I recited the poem, *Life For me Ain't Been No Crystal Stair* by Langston Hughes and won first place. That was real to me. Ugh; just the mere thought of Nancy, my so-called mother, made me cringe.

I closed my eyes again in my room to get some more rest, but it was disturbed by those childhood memories that still haunted me.

Chapter 8- Remembering the Tragedy

As my alarm went off, I turned over to see my mother lying in Tyler's bed. *Oh hell,* I thought. When I went to sleep last night, she wasn't home, but I wasn't surprised. She was always absent, so it didn't shock me anymore. I was twelve years into her psychotic selfish

68

sporadic behavior. It was so frustrating too because to look at Nancy you would think she was a supermodel. She was beautiful on the outside with light brown skin, long wavy hair, an absolutely drop dead gorgeous coca cola bottle figure, and a vocabulary that would impress all the intellectuals. She could give Cornel West a run for his money with her extensive vocabulary. That is probably why she lasted so long in her 'boosting' profession. By the time anyone realized they'd been robbed, Nancy was months long gone, and they would never have suspected that it was her. *What a waste*, I would think so many mornings as I watched her sleep in the bed next to me. She couldn't go to her own huge master bed because my father had her on a curfew. Isn't that the craziest shit you ever heard of? A forty-year-old woman on a curfew. Who does that? Why would anyone have to go to those drastic measures?

This morning was different though. She looked really out of it, and as I looked around for Tyler, I saw him on the top bunk with Ashanti. They were both sound asleep. I rose very quietly and went to Baby Dylan's crib to see that it was empty. Although it was nine of us siblings in this four-bedroom two-bathroom house, most of us like to sleep in the same room. So last night at headcount, we had

Olivia, Joshua, Matthew, Tyler, Ashanti, Zachariah, Sadey, Dylan, and me.

Olivia and Joshua were fraternal twins and the oldest at the age of fourteen while Matthew and I were Irish twins because we were born in the same calendar year and less than 12 months apart. Tyler was ten, Ashanti & Zachariah, mom's next set of fraternal twins were eight, and the cutest of us all was Ms. Sadey Mae at five. Our best gift ever was Baby Dylan at four months.

We all took a serious interest in making sure Baby Dylan was safe at all times. Because Dad was our workingman and the rock of our family, so we did everything we could to help him. We all made sure that we did what we were supposed to. We were really good kids up to that day.

As I looked around in each bed for Baby Dylan, I did not see him. We knew he wasn't in Dad's room because he left for work at 4 a.m. in order to get to the docs by 5 a.m. He was a longshoreman and had been all of our lives. You would think that made us super wealthy, but Nancy had a real gift for blowing every cent of Dad's hard earned money.

As I scanned a second time around the room, I see what I think is Baby Dylan's little footie, but it couldn't be. No, it couldn't be. I froze in shock and horror as I realized that what I see is real. "Olivia! Olivia get up!" I run into the other bedroom to get my older sister because she and Joshua had fallen asleep in the other room down the hall.

"Olivia! Olivia, come quick come quick!" She jumped up out of the bed and tries to calm me down.

"What, Nyla, what? It's Saturday. It's my day to sleep late. Bell, what do you want?"

"Olivia, its Baby Dylan. Mom is... mom is…please, come." I begin to strong-arm pull her to the room for her to see what I can't get out of my head.

Unwillingly, Olivia comes screaming at me along the way until she reaches the doorway. She drops to her knees in terror and I slide down the wall outside because I can't look at it again. That scene was set forever in our minds.

After a few seconds, which seemed like eternity, Olivia looks at me and says, "Nyla…" I don't respond…

"Nyla, get up, shut up! Stop crying. Go downstairs and call 911." I ran downstairs to do what Olivia asked me, but since it was a cordless phone, I ran back upstairs with the phone. I see Tyler, Ashanti, and Zachariah coming out of the room headed downstairs. I heard Olivia telling them to get up and go downstairs and start breakfast. As I come back to the door, I look in to see Olivia, with all of her strength rolling our mother over. I lost it again. Baby Dylan lying there breathless looking like a frozen toy doll. Even with all the screaming and rolling, Mom still didn't get up. I run over to her with the phone still in my hand and try to shake her as Olivia picks up Baby Dylan and just holds him and sobs on him as if her tears had special healing powers to breathe life back into his cold body.

When mom opens her eyes, she leap up so fast that she hit her head on the ceiling fan. She was definitely up then.

"Oh my God! Oh my God! Dylan! Dylan! Baby Dylan! Please baby please! Olivia give me your brother! Give him to me!" At that moment, the sirens are blaring outside and Olivia turns with Baby Dylan still in her arms and runs downstairs to meet the emergency team outside in the parking lot.

"My brother, my brother! Please save my brother. He's not breathing. Please save my brother he's not breathing," Olivia and I both shout. The team swiftly in the

gentlest way takes Baby Dylan into the ambulance and begins to work on him.

"Young ladies, please, where are your parents?"

At that moment our mother runs outside and starts screaming and wailing and screaming and wailing. "Please save my baby! Please save my baby!"

Olivia and I are screaming in unison, "Dylan wake up. Wake up Dylan. Dylan wake up!"

Chapter 9- First Time for Everything

Still screaming Dylan's name, hysterically, I jumped up out of my sleep. I was dripping in sweat, absolutely soaked from head to toe. This was the first time that I had to wake myself up. It was unbearable. When I realized that I was in my dorm room, I didn't feel any more relieved. I frantically searched around my room for something, anything to calm me down. It used to be Olivia or my Dad who would come and wake me up from those horrible nightmares, but neither of them could be here to sooth me.

Some people thought that I should be handling it all better, but this just happened six years ago. My brother's death was a traumatic experience, and then I had to bury another sibling soon after that. No, the shit wasn't easy at all.

Everything that happened after the paramedics came to try and save my brother that night was a blur. Even after six years and to this very moment, I still couldn't cry enough. There definitely weren't enough tears to cry for my other love. It seemed like yesterday that we buried Baby Dylan and our lives would never be the same. The months after his death were some of the worse, and we all had to endure it. All of us did endure it, except for my trifling self-centered ass mother. After the courts ruled it an accident, she was free and clear to go run the streets as she always did when things had become too stressful for her.

Now friend, I know you are probably doing the math by now and you can see that I received a scholarship for being from a large family while if we took Baby Dylan out because he's in heaven now, we would still be a large family of ten. Well it has been an emotional time and I'm not ready to talk about that other tragedy that wrecked our family and left us with two less Howard children. That is a story for another day, Friend.

But I will tell you that, it used to be Rashad's voice on the phone or body next to me that could help me during these times, but I no longer had that to count on since he

74

was a lying sack of shit. I kept searching for my big sister Olivia's senior cheerleading sweatshirt. Her sweatshirt always gave me strength and comfort during these times. Once I found it and held it close, I could hear her in my mind saying, 'Breathe, Bell, breathe.' She always called me Bell and only she could calm me down when my father wasn't there to help me.

Just as I got my breathing under control and wiped my eyes, my dorm room phone rang. Thank God my roommate and new bestie Sharon stayed over to her new boo thang's house because she didn't know about my family history, and I was not ready to tell her any of it.

"Hello?"

"Good morning, Nyla."

Oh my God, it's Jeffrey! I screamed inside. This must be a sign. He's calling me right in my most needed hour. *Is this a sign God? Is he The One for me?* I snapped myself out of that line of thinking and answered in a very cavalier manner.

"Hello. Who am I speaking with?" I was playing hard to get as if I couldn't pick his voice out of a room full of one hundred people.

"It's Jeffrey, your personal Student Ambassador."

"Oh, hi. Good morning, Jeffrey and stop it. You're the entire freshman class Student Ambassador."

"Yes, but I'm your personal one. What are you doing?"

He's so damn confident, and I love it.

"Nothing right now. I just woke up and was contemplating what I was going to do for the day. I think I might just go to the library and see what new books are out to read."

"Wow, Nyla I love that about you. You're so different. It's one of the important rival football games of the season, and you're spending it at the library. How great is that."

"Um, Jeffery, are you making fun of me? It sounds like you are because I love football. I'm just not in the mood to go out to watch the game."

"Blasphemy, I say! What could make anyone not want to watch THIS game- especially when it is FSU versus UF? Besides University of Miami, UF is one of our biggest rivals!"

Just the mention of University of Miami sent me into a different headspace. One that made me think about Rashad's cheating ass and my plans to make him pay for what he had done to me, to us, to our future and dreams.

Ugh. It made me almost explode, but I held it together long enough to respond.

"Well, I have my reasons Jeffrey. Umm, can you call me back some other time? I appreciate your Saturday ambassador phone call, but I'm going to hang up now?"

"Okay, Nyla I understand. I'll definitely see you later."

"Goodbye, Jeffery. See you later."

I couldn't help but smile through the pain. My own personal student ambassador wasn't so bad. Jeffrey was a breath of fresh air in my current dark smog.

*

I got completely out of bed to try and start my Saturday, but it was no use. I was in a funk. At that moment, the phone rings again. I ignore it this time. Somebody really wanted to talk to us because they kept calling over and over again. I know some people thought we were crazy for having a dorm room phone, but we liked it. It made us feel important. I hated talking on the phone, so I barely knew where my cell phone was located; if anyone really wanted to talk to me they knew how to find me.

Finally, I answer the phone to my crazy ass friend and roommate Sharon.

"Girl, why haven't you been answering the phone?"

"Umm, maybe because I was sleep. What's up girl?"

"Listen, so Roger is having a football party and wanted you to come over. I have to come home and change, so I can pick you up. Game starts at 4pm, so I'll be there about 2pm to pick you up. You down?"

"Sharon, as cool as that sounds, I'll have to pass. I'm tired and really feel like being alone."

"Usually, I would try and convince you by begging and pleading, but I can hear in your voice that you're not going to be persuaded this time, so OKAY for now."

"Okay, girl I'll see you when you get here. Bye."

"Bye, little old lady. See you in a little bit. Hopefully, you'll change your mind when I get there."

"Probably not," I said as I hung up the phone.

Since we first met at orientation earlier last summer, Sharon and I had become extremely close. She was a fun carefree person. She was from Tampa and came from a very good home from what I could tell. Her parents had been married for thirty plus years and seemed to be very happy together. They had very high expectations of her, and she didn't seem to mind or let it affect her in any negative ways. Sharon was always a happy person and she loved to have fun. It didn't seem like she allowed anything to bother her or get in her way. She had everything, and she didn't have to share it with anyone because she was an only child. I could tell that there was a lot more to Sharon than she let on; however, just like I would share in my own time, I could respect her if she wanted to share her life in her own time. We were from two different worlds, but we still had a lot in common. We both loved to travel and enjoyed school. I believe school came easier to me, but she enjoyed it just the same. We spent a lot of time talking about life and our visions for our futures and the places we wanted to go with the people we wanted to meet. Hell we talked about any and everything, but didn't get deep into family stuff.

I wasn't ready to share with her my family dynamics or the pain and losses of my past, so I often times just listened to all of her childhood memories and stories. She was much more of a talker than I was so it was easy to ask her questions and just let her go on and on. I didn't want to spoil her weekend, so I didn't tell her about Rashad either. Honestly, she probably would have been happy about it. She always told me long distance wouldn't work, but I was so determined to make her a believer in true love.

That bastard made me fail at that, too. I promise his ass was going to pay for this shit.

After another ten minutes, I finally got out of the bed and went to take a shower and get dressed for my day. Rashad had tried calling me last night and this morning, but I ignored his calls. I just wanted to go and wash the pain of yesterday away once and for all.

By the time I gathered myself and looked presentable for the library, it was already noon and I had not eaten anything. Just as I was packing my backpack, there was a knock at my door. I chuckled inside and thought hmm seems clothes wasn't the only thing Sharon forgot, so I opened the door to see Mr. Student Ambassador, Jeffrey Donovan, standing there with his face painted like a typical FSU radical football fan and a big alluring smile.

"Hello, Nyla. I said you'd be seeing me later, so now is later."

I could not do anything except shake my head. "Jeffrey, you are truly persistent. You are really ready for the game aren't you?"

"I have to be Nyla. I live for FSU football season!" Jeffrey was a junior engineering major from Quincy, FL, which was about thirty minutes away from Tallahassee, so it seemed like he knew everything about everything in

Tallahassee. I remember thinking at orientation how knowledgeable he was about the area.

"Well, Jeffrey. I actually love football too. I just wasn't in the mood today."

"What's up? You want to talk about it? What's wrong?"

"My goodness, you're mighty inquisitive I'll say."

"It's my duty as your personal student ambassador. I have to check on you. I didn't like the way you sounded earlier especially when you said you're not watching the game, so I brought you some food to see if I could convince you."

Oh yes, goodness, food! I thought as I just stared at him in disbelief.

"May I come in please?"

"Oh my goodness, you sure can come in." I didn't even realize I had him standing outside all this time with food and his charming personality. Our dorm was co-ed so we could have the opposite sex in our rooms. They just couldn't stay overnight.

"I brought you some wings and buffalo shrimp from BW3 along with some of your favorites. I hope you enjoy them."

"Wait, my favorites. What favorites?"

"Remember the icebreaker we did at orientation", he asked? Well I remember you saying your favorite candies were pull & peel cherry Twizzlers and chocolate covered raisins. I hope I got the right ones. I never realized how many different varieties of Twizzlers were out there. I hope that wasn't too much."

"No, it wasn't too much at all, thank you Jeffrey. That was super thoughtful."

"I really want you to come with me to the game. If you don't want to go to the game, we can go to my place and watch it on my big screen TV. My roommate will be at the game, so you can still have your alone vibe if you like. I won't even talk to you, if you don't mind me screaming at the TV every once in a while."

He was the perfect damn gentleman. He opened car doors, let me walk in first, held my hand and was such a nice guy.

Jeffrey lived in a gorgeous apartment/townhouse subdivision with gorgeously manicured landscaping and complex features. When you drove in through the gates, there was a welcome sign that lit up with bold bright colors that said welcome back neighbor. As we approached his residence, I began to feel a little nervous. I did not know what to expect. What if he didn't clean up? Hell what if he was into S&M and was luring me into a sexual trap? I chuckled at myself because he certainly didn't seem like the type to have to lure anyone anywhere. I would have come willing to anything he asked me to right now.

Once we got to his townhouse, I was stuffed with wings and shrimp and some of my Twizzlers on the ride over. I just couldn't stop smiling because he actually convinced me to come. His actions made me forget about Rashad for a moment. Jeffrey seemed so into me.

As we walked into his apartment, my cell started to ring. I looked down and it was Sharon of course.

"Umm, where the hell are you?" She actually sounded concerned.

"Oh, I'm sorry. I forgot to leave a note. Jeffrey came over and convinced me to watch the game. I'm at his place."

"What! Okay, then girl okay then!" Her smile was beaming through the phone.

"Whatever, Sharon! We're just going to watch the game at his place."

"Girl, I'm not even mad at you, she exclaimed! I would have ditched me for Mr. Caramel too. But what about Rashad, the love of your life; the flame in your heart; the fire in your soul?"

"Fuc…" I almost went off, but I just stopped myself. "That's over. I'll have to give you that story later this weekend. See you later."

"Ugh, Nyla. Don't do that to me. You know I want to know. What the hell happened? Do we need to take a trip to Miami?"

"See, this is why I love you girl! You are always ready to ride! But no, I am fine for now. I'll tell you about it later."

Jeffrey, did not appear to be alarmed or bothered at all by our conversation. He just showed me into his apartment and to the couch where I sat to finish my conversation with Sharon.

After I hung up with her, he immediately pulled me up off the couch and gave me a big sexy close hug. I could feel every pack in what seemed like his 12 pack abs ripped stomach. I could feel his broad shoulders and- oh my goodness- I could feel his Mr. Brown Downtown. I let him hold me and just sank into his arms. His embrace was electrifying. I felt alive and fearless in his arms.

"I just thought you needed that," he whispered to me as he looked into my eyes as if I was the only girl on this earth that he needed and wanted.

I returned his gaze, and as he went in for a kiss on my lips, I closed my eyes ready for the embrace, but was a little disappointed to feel his luscious lips on my cheek then forehead.

What a gentleman! Oh my, I could love this boy!

He pulled back from me just a little bit, took my hand and gave me a tour of the downstairs.

For a college student, his place was super nice. I mean it was dope for real. Every room was painted a different color. The walls in his living room were a calm light gold, almost cream color with a chocolate accent wall. His furniture definitely complimented the room with its chocolate leather tones to highlight the khaki colored furniture. He had this gorgeous multicolored lounge chair that was absolutely stunning. It had all shades of brown, black, purple and gold tones to it. It was nestled in the corner as if only a certain select few were allowed to sit in it.

The dining room was another gold toned color with a deep purple accent wall. The wall was so beautiful because it was uniquely painted to look like a swirl of purple and gold tones. It was nice. His kitchen was nice with an island in the center and gorgeous granite countertops along with stainless steel appliances with yet another beautiful gold color tone to his walls. This man truly knew how to decorate, even though some areas definitely seemed like they had a woman's touch. I just assumed that his mother or some female family member helped them.

This place must cost a fortune, but probably because it was in Tallahassee, and everything was cheaper in Tallahassee compared to Miami.

He led me to the door that led to his outside area, and though small, it was so nice and peaceful outside. He had a covered patio that he made look serene with a swing patio two seater, cute FSU lounge chairs and a grill in the far corner to demonstrate that barbecuing was always an option at his place. There was two of everything, and I kept thinking gosh he and his roommate must be really close.

There were decorative art pieces and figurines all around his home that further demonstrated his sexiness. I was just more and more impressed with this man. His taste was surprisingly unique. It was evident why he would pick such an area a little further away from campus than most. This place was nice. I mean really nice. Did I say *nice*?

He led me back past the living room into another room on the other side of the front door. The sign on the door was a signature piece and read "Only Loyal Seminole Fans Allowed" with a Seminole head to the right and left of the words. As we walked into the room, you could feel the FSU Seminole spirit present. If you weren't in the spirit when you entered, you certainly were by the time you walked around this room. He had a sectional that had theater style reclining seats at each end with cup holders in the armrests. The walls were garnet and gold all around with one wall that had the same swirl pattern but with garnet and gold this time. The game would be playing on the huge 72-inch flat screen that was mounted on the wall. There was a pool table over to in the right corner, and more chairs in different variations all around the room. This was the perfect game watching spot. There was a classic bar in the left corner of the room that had shelves built to hold a variety of alcoholic beverages from Hennessey to Crown Royal to Titos Vodka and Kettle One. He even had a nice variety of wines in all colors. No one was left out. In a medium six-beer refrigerator to the right of the bar, he had Heinekens and Coronas. It was clear what beer and alcohol he liked and he offered me a glass, but I declined at that time.

On the bar top, he had everything you needed. I looked around the back to see every type of glass from wine glasses to margarita glasses to martini glasses to beer mugs to shot glasses to nice small glasses to have your wine as you smoked your cigar. Yes this FSU junior, soon to be senior in the spring, had a nice collection of cigars. They ranged from Cubans to Rocky Patel.

As I smiled at the décor, I turned to see the game and hear the cheers. We had just scored another touchdown and the score was now 21 to 3 FSU.

"Beat that azz down! He screamed at the TV. Beat that azz!"

I loved a man who loved their sports. It was so sexy, so I didn't show him how much I knew about football. I just smiled and said, "Yes we are beating them good!"

By half time, I was beginning to get sleepy, so I did take a nap on his lap. As he stroked my hair and rubbed my face, I drifted off to sleep. By the time fourth quarter was almost over, I lifted up to see the score.

"Hell, yeah!" We beat them good. Jeffrey just smiled and continued to rub my face. As I looked into his memorizing hazel eyes, I knew I was in trouble.

He reached in to kiss me and I did not object. It felt so good and I wanted more. I wanted so much more, but I stopped him.

"Jeffrey, yesterday was rough for me. I found out my boyfriend is cheating on me, and I don't want to blur the lines between us by doing something with you I will regret."

"Nyla, that clown is an idiot. Anyone that would cheat on you is a fucking fool. I'm sorry that happened, but I can't say that I'm not happy about it. Ever since I laid eyes on you at orientation, I have not been able to stop thinking about you. I want you so bad in any way that I can have you."

As he said that, he slid down on his knees in front of me, raised my khaki skirt that matched perfectly with my new FSU fitted tee, and began to kiss all over my lower parts. He lifted and rested my legs ever so gently on his shoulders and proceeded to take me to another world. Dammit, a world I had never been to before. He made me scream pleasures and obscenities all at the same time. I called for him in pure lust, love, and sincerity. It felt like he had two tongues and they were both working at different speeds in a pattern that would make me cum over and over again. He knew what the hell he was doing and it showed.

He didn't pull too hard or suck too much. He was careful and dedicated to his work- me.

"Oh my gosh, Nyla. I knew you would taste so good like nothing I have ever tasted before. I just want to please you. I just want to please you. Damn- I am so into you. Shit! You taste so delicious."

I couldn't respond. I was still recuperating from the third orgasm I just had that wet up his entire upper and lower lips. I was in vagina paradise. This man was freaking amazing.

He came up on me slowly with every part of my body feeling his kisses. When he reached my lips, he asked if he could kiss me there. I did not respond with words but put my lips on his in passion and lust and urgency.

I had never felt this way before. Rashad and I had come to this point, but he was so fast and forceful. Jeffrey took his damn time and made it last. I didn't want to tell him I was still a virgin, so I let him feel me in every way he wanted to because I wanted it so bad. I wanted him so bad.

"Nyla, we can go upstairs if you want?"

I straddled him and he picked me up. With my legs wrapped around his waist, he carried me towards the door passionately kissing me every step of the way. My mind was telling me to stop him before we went up the stairs, but my body choked her until she stopped thinking at all. My body and heart were in complete control at this point.

His room was a definite panty dropper. The walls were painted a deep gold with one cream accent wall with decorative gorgeous artwork all around. This damn man loved purple and gold. He had a huge king slay bed that sat up high with a gorgeous satin gold bed set. His chocolate and purple pillows were the perfect blend of masculinity and style that any man could show and anyone woman would love. He had me. I was under his spell.

As he gently placed me on the bed, he never took his eyes off of me. I felt so important, so special.

"Jeffrey, please slow, I've never..." His eyes stayed focused on me as if he felt completely honored to be my first.

As he spoke, his words were so sincere, and touched me so deeply. "Nyla, I won't hurt you. Trust me."

I did. I did trust him.

That man licked me again. Dammit, he paid attention to the details and took value in his work- ME. He sucked my breast with smooth caress. He massaged them and gently sucked them and before, after and during his moves, he always made eye contact. He turned me over and kissed me from the very top of my head to the tip of my feet. He did not miss any part of my body. I tried to return some of the kisses, but he declined in such a gentleman like manner.

"Nyla, tonight is only for you. I want to satisfy you like you've never been satisfied before. Just enjoy it. I promise I'll enjoy myself, too."

Holy shit, I kept thinking. *This man is trying to make me crazy over him.*

As he came to his knees in front of me, he pulled me up to look into his eyes, and he said, "Nyla, I love you. From the first day I saw you it was love at first sight. If you don't want to go any further, we don't have to. I will be here after this night until you tell me to go away."

Oh my goodness. Before I knew it, tears were in my eyes streaming down my face. How could this man feel so deeply for me? From orientation to this current day, it had been five months and three days that he knew me. During that time, he always found a way to be on my mind.

At first, it was the generic emails that he would send to his entire small group, and then he would send me individual emails.

I could not believe what I was hearing, but I had to remember the door I needed to close with Rashad and probably the time I needed to heal and reflect before I began a relationship with Jeffrey.

So against what me and my Virginia Brown wanted to do, I said "Jeffery, yes, let's stop. I have to get out of one thing before I can think about starting another." He complied, but still made that night amazing. He just held me and we talked all night long.

I told him about my family and all the dysfunctional dynamics. I promise it looked like he shed a couple of tears, but I learned a lot about him, too. He was from a very close knit family. He had three sisters and no brothers. His family had their own construction business, and they were very well known in Quincy and all surrounding areas-including Tallahassee. His parents were both from large families, so all the full-time employees of their company were related in some way.

His family's business was the construction of mostly commercial properties or subdivisions such as the one he lived in. Oh, I thought. That explains how he could afford such a nice place in such a beautiful community. That could also explain where his impeccable taste came from as well. He said he was really close to his mother and father, which surprised me because you know my family history. I'm not close to my mother at all.

93

We snuggled like we were in love and at some points I thought I could have been in love with him, but I had to keep denying myself because I kept remembering and being aggravated by the thoughts of Rashad.

Chapter 10- Keeping My Secret, Writing My Pain

Oh the shit hit me like a ton of bricks in the shower that Monday morning after the initial discovery. Even after three days, I was still pissed, hurt, and just completely consumed with this pain. I tried to write, which is what I do when I am feeling emotional. I wrote so many pieces about him that it made me sick.

Low life, low life- how dare you be?
You have the nerve to actually cheat on me.
My cup runneth over for you, and I let you inside.
I made you my man even though you won't subside.
You call me into a world of lust and sweat. Low life
where's your conscience? You don't have one, I bet.

I would write several pieces about that jerk but they did not equate to the number of pieces I put up for Jeffrey, but it is still time to make him pay. Rashad had the nerve, the downright audacity to cheat on me. It is time to make him pay- that is all I kept thinking.

I could not help but reminisce on the nature and essence of our relationship. It was the typical 'good woman help her man' experience. I helped this man through high school. He gladly accepted. He definitely took care of me financially, and I never had to worry about anything. But surely he could not have thought that he could just do whatever because of that little bit of money. I had my own money. I could take care of myself. Shit, I started working at fourteen and knew the importance of a dollar. I would lie to my mother about my paycheck, so I didn't have to give her the entire thing. I would save some money to get my necessities and some of my wants. Working for a check felt like the best form of independence, so I learned very early that a man had to provide more than I could for myself. That man had to be ready to provide for me. My money would be to support my siblings and his to support me. It seemed like the perfect concept and plan. It was too bad Rashad didn't get the memo that told him his duties. That motherfucker had the nerve to cheat on me, so his ass gotta learn on this day. So… what could I do to make him feel like I do?

Men love their cars, money, and our female Virginias. Since he messed with my heart and soul, I believe it only fair to destroy the things he held so dear. I was going home for thanksgiving break in three weeks, so I could strike then.

After my night with Jeffrey, I decided not to tell Rashad just yet that I knew about his cheating ass, so he still had no idea that I knew about Wanda's skinny ass and the others I heard about after Wanda. My girl Kendra became a private eye at UM. She found out so much about Rashad and his escapades. That bastard was all over South Florida fucking in every area code from 305 to 786 to 954 and on. He even had a few in North Florida's 352 and 904 area code. It seemed like he was all up I-95 dropping penis all on the way. The more I thought about it the more I was ready and convinced: Rashad must pay and pay well.

Chapter 11- Is it Love?

As I fumbled with the keys to get into my dorm room, I could hear Sharon on the other side heading to the door. Dammit, hurry up and open before this nut embarrasses you, Nyla. Too late.

She swings the door open in full big sister mode. "Um, excuse me sir! What time is it? Hell we can forget that. What day is it?"

"Hi, Sharon." Jeffrey said with the coolness of Denzel Washington.

She certainly calmed down like most women would if Denzel were talking to them. "Good morning, Jeffrey. My girl better still be a woman of virtue."

"Yes, Sharon she certainly is."

We all chuckled and all I could do is shake my head. Sharon is absolutely crazy.

"Umm, mama, now that you know I am still a woman of virtue, can I have some privacy to say goodbye to Jeffrey?" I asked as if she really was my mother.

"I guess," she chuckled and walked away.

I turned to Jeffrey who was staring at me already and before I could say a word, his lips were embracing mine as if it was our first kiss and he had been waiting years to have my lips.

It caught me off guard, but I welcomed every bit of his embrace.

"Nyla. Thank you for a night that I will never forget. You are one of a kind, and I truly don't want to mess things up with you. I know that you have some

97

unresolved things to handle, and I don't want to pressure you, so I will step to the side and give you your space. But know that I want you. I want all of you inside and out."

His proclamation was sealed with one of the most passionate kisses I have ever had.

"Yes sir." That was all I could muster up to say out of my mouth.

"I will call you later. Okay?"

"Yes. That is fine."

As soon as that girl heard the door shut, she was right in front of me as if she had magical powers to just appear. "Okay. Girl! What happened? I want all the damn details. Don't leave anything out. I'm serious. Tell it all, Bitch!"

"Now, Sharon. You know I don't kiss and tell."

"Girl, forget that. You better kiss and scream for me! Cuz honey my night was a damn wrap. I can't stand a fool that can't hold his liquor. That damn man was too big to get drunk off a couple shots of tequila! Girl, I ended up doctoring his sick ass all night. What a damn waste of my time, so spill the beans sista!"

"Sharon, it was magical! That is the best way to describe it. I could love that man forever."

As I walked past her into our room, I left her with her mouth hung down and open. Now she knew how I felt, and I did feel that way for a few weeks.

Chapter 12- My Boo

Jeffrey called me all the time. We talked all the time. He would come by and walk me to class. He would take me to lunch at places I knew I shouldn't be eating like Bennigan's, Olean's Soul Food, Blue Collar Cafe, Shingles Chicken, and Guthrie's. Now Guthrie's was one of my favorites. Those chicken fingers were the best in the world, and I literally mean the whole planet earth. The 'gut' box was like no other.

I loved when Jeffrey would just call and say, 'Let's go eat. You have time?"

I always had time for him, and I would always eat and enjoyed every bite of every meal we shared together. Thank God I took my student fees seriously and utilized our award winning state of the art Fitness Center. If I didn't work out five to six times a week, I would have been a huge cow because Jeffrey believed in feeding me both mentally and physically.

"So Nyla, if you could live anywhere in the world where would it be?" He asked as we sipped our milkshakes and shared a Monte Cristo sandwich and fries at Bennigan's.

"It would probably be an island like Jamaica or the Bahamas. I love the beach and it seems like they have no worries there. I told my friends I want to go to Jamaica for our spring break because I really want to experience the island life."

"Okay. I can see us living in Jamaica," he said.

"Okay, Jeffrey. Us?" I replied trying not to smile too hard.

"Yes, Nyla Bell. Us. You, me, and the five kids and two dogs that we will have. Us."

As he smiled, so did I until we were both blushing.

Jeffrey knew how to turn on his charm and make me fall deeper and deeper into his love. That damn man was determined to get close to me. It was so obvious to everyone, but we still weren't a couple, and that kept me on my toes.

Sharon would always ask me what we were waiting on, and I would simply tell her. "I'm waiting on him, and he's waiting on time."

Her reply would always be, "What the hell does that mean?"

My answer would be the same every time, "I don't know. Just like I don't know what he is waiting on."

He had plenty of reasons and none of them seemed good enough for me, so I thought about the positive and didn't focus on that part, but I am nobody's fool. So, I kept my wall up because I couldn't give him everything without that commitment and title.

YES, Friend! I needed the title! Fuck what people say! He did all the things I would want my man to do. He called consistently, had things to talk about, made me laugh, loved and cherished his mother, liked to do different things, could swim, loved to travel, was sexy and handsome as hell, adored me, and loved God. We had been to church a few times together, so I know that he is a Believer. He just wouldn't make it official, and that made me nervous. Like, he wanted me, but had something or someone else he didn't want to get rid of. I'm sorry for all of those who don't need the title because yes, and yes again, I need and must have it. So, when he asked me to the Black Student Union Ball, I said no.

When I told Kendra, she dropped the phone.

"You did what Nyla?"

"Yes girl, I said no. I've decided to pull back and protect my heart. I want him to be my man, but I'm not forcing him. But girl you know the saying "why buy the cow if you can get the milk for free?" "So while he continues to shop, I'll be on the shelf collecting more value and remaining available for other possible male buyers."

"I hear you Ny: I hear you." Ken sounded unconvinced.

I continued, "Now, pick up your face and close your mouth. Yes, you damn right. I said no, so when you coming?"

*

I like that the plan was made for my girls and I to go to the ball together. We had a freakin' blast at the ball, we truly did!

We went as an All Girls Posse that included myself, Sharon, Kendra, and Joy. We dressed in all black and silver gowns with diamond accessories and variations of stilettos. I bought all of us corsages, and I wore my hair in a half up half down curly style, so you could still see my accessories. It truly was a shimmering affair. We danced ourselves into complete sweats at the Ball. We partied from Thursday after our last classes to Monday morning just in time to go to our Monday morning classes.

Kendra came up from Miami and stayed the whole week and entire weekend with us. Her school is private, so they had the week off for something or another. So, she went to classes with me and got to experience the Union on Wednesdays first hand. She was just as amazed by all the action in the Union as I was that first week of school. Unlike me, she did not stay away from the football section and ended up with one of their numbers. Sharon met us in the Union after her class, and when she heard about her and Mr. Football, she gave her the same speech she gave me during orientation.

"Hey, at least she was consistent," I chuckled and said when Kendra looked at me puzzled about why Sharon was in Big Sister mode.

Chapter 13- Ayee! Homecoming, Baby!

"IT'S HOMECOMING WEEK BITCHES!" That's all you heard throughout our dorm and all over campus. This was one of the most exciting times of the year, and I just have to say thank you for Tallahassee and football. It was a great distraction from all the mess going on in my life. Homecoming was a time for all past and present students to come to FSU and celebrate another year of being a Seminole. There was always an official homecoming week of celebrations, but that certainly wasn't enough for the massive amounts of people that would come to town to celebrate. There were so many different groups that would have homecoming schedules of festivities. The fraternities and sororities had special events for their members and guests. The Alumni associations had a host of events for their members and guests. The great thing about it was that you could literally have something to do from the time you got up until the time you went to sleep. No matter what time that was, somewhere in Tallahassee was a place to party homecoming style, and I was ready for it all.

Of course, the Monday of Homecoming week was supposed to be business as usual. You were expected to go to class, study, and get ready for the upcoming weekend, but some people on and off campus defied those expectations with pop up parties and socials. Some of those socials had alcohol while others didn't, but either way, it was destined to be a good time. Tuesday night was BW3 night with 25-cent wings and drink specials. You were always certain to meet somebody on wing night. It was like a magnet for people to meet up, hook up, and have a blast. Wednesday was the Stateroom party on campus and the Homecoming Concert at the Civic center. If you planned it right, you could go to both of them and enjoy every minute. We had Dave Chappelle as a headliner for the Civic Center. I had to make that event, and the Stateroom party was just about music and dancing so hard until you came out of there soaking wet from sweat, so you had to dress accordingly. I don't know what everybody else was doing or what was scheduled, but Thursday was a preparation and rest day for me.

I went to class, slept, and studied the entire day. My dad never had to worry about me. He always said that he was proud of my ability to prioritize and manage my time. I didn't like getting into trouble or being told what to do, so I tried to do what I was supposed to, so that I could do what I wanted to do at all times. I remember my brother Josh being so mad at me because he and Ty always knew how sneaky I was, but I never got caught. Josh stayed in trouble, and I used to tell him it was because he didn't know how to balance. See, Josh only wanted to do what he wanted to do, so he kept a lot of attention on himself. I tried to help him, but he was hard headed. So he stayed on punishment while Ty and I would be all over town all the time.

On another note, Rashad and Jeffery were still somewhere rolling around in the very back of my mind. But, I didn't want to focus on them. They were downers, and I wanted to live my best life on the up and up! Eventually, I would have to deal with both of them.

*

Since FAMU's homecoming had just ended, I was still in party mode and ready to keep the party going. With the new friends I met from FAMU's homecoming, I had the rest of my social calendar booked until my sophomore year. The weekend after our homecoming we already had plans to go to Atlanta for AUC homecoming festivities. The AUC was the Atlanta University Center, which consisted of Clark Atlanta University, Spelman College, Morehouse College, and Morehouse School of Medicine. That would be more men than we knew what to do with, and I was ready for them all.

FSU homecoming was the best, and I am not just saying that because I was a Seminole. Well maybe I am, but we had the most fun at FSU's homecoming. I think it was because none of us were expecting it. We knew we were in the minority, but everything from the Step Show in the union to the parade on Friday to the tailgate and the pop up parties all around town was dope. We had a freakin blast.

"Hey girl! Excuse me. Can I talk to you?" a group of guys screamed from one truck.

Of course we all ignored them, but it was funny nonetheless.

A few steps down Pensacola Street was another group of guys with their salutations, and yet again, we gave quick hellos and kept walking. No one had caught our attention yet, but it was just noon, and we hadn't been out of car for ten minutes. Then as we headed into the stadium parking lot, a group of *real men* knew exactly what to say.

"Excuse me. Your hands are empty- would you all like a drink?"

Ding ding ding. Those were the magic words and music to our ears, so we walked on closer and into the Black Alumni tailgate.

"Hi, how are you? I'm Rod."

We all spoke and shook our escort, Rod's hand.

"What are your names?"

"I'm Sharon."

"I'm Joy, and this is Nyla," Joy said as if I couldn't speak for myself.

I simply smiled and waved, and there he was- Jeffery. I hadn't spoken to him for about two weeks at this point. He was upset because I would not go to the ball with him, and I was upset because he wouldn't make things official with us, so we just didn't speak.

As I turned to walk away before he saw me, it was too late and there he was- right there in front of me.

"Hi Nyla."

"Hello Jeffrey."

"I've been thinking about you. How are you? I've missed you."

"I've been good. Just busy with school and all."

"I've missed you," he repeated.

"Yes, I heard you the first time you said it, but I haven't had any missed calls or messages from you."

"I know, but that doesn't change the fact that I have missed you. I've wanted to call every day since that day."

"And yet you didn't."

"Because I didn't know what to say, but I have missed you and I can't stop thinking about you. Can we go somewhere and talk?"

"What, are you crazy? It's the middle of homecoming, Jeffrey. We can certainly talk later."

"Okay, Nyla, but know that my feelings get deeper for you each day and I miss you each day that I am away from you."

I just stared at him in complete disbelief and was mad at myself because I believed him. I believed every word that flowed from his mouth. I knew that he loved me for real so I had to fight the feelings to always forgive him.

"Enjoy homecoming," I said as I turned and walked away.

I wish I could tell you that he let me walk away without a fight, but I can't because he didn't.

"Nyla," he called and the next thing you know, he was in front of me again on his knees, both knees, in the middle of the tailgate party.

"Oh my goodness, Jeffrey get up right now."

"Only if you agree to go somewhere and talk to me," he said while still on his knees in front of me.

"Okay, okay. Just please get up now." With one quick motion he was up and had my hand leading me away from the party.

We talked through most of the game, and it wasn't until my girls came looking for me that we released from our embrace.

"Um, Nyla. We have been looking for your ass for the past thirty minutes. Bring yo ass girl. We at least want to go into the game that were paid for by our student fees for a little while."

"Okay, Sharon. I'm coming."

She came by herself while Joy waited in the distance but was staring at us the entire time.

"Jeffrey, I will talk to you later," I said as he continued to hold my hand as I turned to walk away.

"Nyla."

"Yes?"

"You know I am in love with you right?"

Sharon just looked at both of us in disgust.

"Yes, Jeffrey. I know." That was the response he needed to let go of my hand and so he did and Sharon and I walked away to meet up with Joy to go into the game.

"Girl, what do y'all have going on? Is he into you or *what*?"

110

"Yes, girl he really is," Joy said agreeing with
Sharon.

"Yes I know, but he must not be too head over heels
because I'm still not his woman." I shrugged my shoulders
and walked past both of them into the security line to enter
the stadium for the game.

Of course, we won the game and celebrated all
night long.

*

The next day we made it to church, but I can't say that I
remembered anything except for the new youth pastor
that was fine as heavens and all things holy. When
Monday rolled around, I felt ready for the week,
especially since it was going to be a three day weekend
and we were going to the AUC homecoming in Atlanta.

Chapter 14- Road Trippin'

When I talked to Kendra that Monday after class,
we were in conference call mode to solidify all of our
plans. On Friday, Kendra would fly back to Tallahassee,
and we would pick her up from the airport and hit the road
headed to Atlanta to make all the festivities. It was such a
well laid out plan. We were all excited. I was super hype

about this road trip. We all went to class on Monday happier than we had ever been because we were looking forward to the weekend of fun and excitement we were about to have in Atlanta.

My girls and I all had pretty rigorous school schedules, but we were determined to be the best students academically and socially. Well, at least I was determined. We had our road trip all planned out and it would go smoothly if we followed the plan. We would take turns driving. There would be two in the back seat studying while the one in the front passenger seat would ride as the Shotgun for the driver. Now, the Shotgun role was critical and that person had to stay up with the driver. They were the extra eyes for the driver and watched for hazards including the cops. I couldn't stress this enough- the Shotgun *had to* stay up. We would only stop for gas and that would be the only time we had to relieve ourselves in the bathroom, stretch, and/or get a snack or two. We would do this same plan there and back, so when Monday hit, it was back to the grind, and we would be ready. There would be no remnants from the weekend, and we would be back in school mode and completely ignorant to anything around us besides the path to class. The plan was air tight, if we followed it, and that was our plan.

112

The next morning though, my excitement was drained from me like blood from a human being sucked by a vampire.

"Girl. It's 8:00 in the morning what is wrong?" I said as my greeting when I picked up the phone.

"I tried calling you last night, but I couldn't reach you. Girl Rashad is ..."

"Rashad is what? Ken you know I hate it when you do this. Rashad is what?"

"Rashad was arrested last night."

"What the hell? For what?"

"I don't know all the charges but he called and asked me to come get him. I tried to call you, but couldn't get you."

"I tried calling Rashad this morning before I headed to my class, and again there was no answer and no return phone call. At least now I know why. What happened?"

"Well, Nyla."

She was stalling and stuttering and she knew how much I hated when she did that.

"Oh my goodness Ken. Just get it out!"

"Nyla. Shany called me to tell me that Rashad and Wanda were caught having sex in the stadium and when the police approached him, Rashad flipped out. I don't know if he was drunk and high, but I definitely know when I picked him up he smelled like he had been drinking for days. Shany said they let Wanda go, but since Rashad kept flipping out they arrested him. When I got down there to pick him up, he told me a completely different story. I know you hate him right now, but I couldn't just leave him in jail especially with him being on this football scholarship."

I just laid there in disbelief.

"This boy just keeps breaking my heart. You would think that I did something wrong to him. The way he was neglecting me was evident that he had his attention, eyes, and dick somewhere else. Yeah, granted I hadn't given it up, but he said he was fine with waiting. He even said he would wait with and for me. Yes, we had been together for a while, but he always made it seem like he didn't want my body over my heart and mind. He always said that.

Rashad would always say, "Nyla. I want to live in your heart and mind. Your body, as fine as it is, can wait. I want to be engraved and woven into your heart, so you beat like I beat and move like I move."

"Well thank God that shit never happened. What a piece of crap. He is a lying sack of horse manure. He deserves to rot. You know what? The AUC homecoming will have to wait. I am coming down there."

"I figured you were going to say that Nyla. That's why I didn't waste my time coming there. See you when you get here. You know I'm ready."

Immediately, I told Sharon what happened, and like I thought, she was down. We asked Joy if she wanted to go, and just like that we were ready to be Miami-bound on a covert operation to fuck Rashad's cheating ass up.

Let's do this, I thought! His ass deserved it. It's about to be a road trip of epic proportions.

Chapter 15- Lord, Have Mercy

The ringing of my dorm room phone interrupted my plotting and planning. I answered with a curt, "Hello?" and was further annoyed to hear my mother on the other end of the phone. I sighed big and braced myself for whatever she was going to say.

"Hi, Nyla. It's your mother."

Huh, I thought. What an overstatement. This woman couldn't be a mother if she tried.

"Is everything okay?" I managed to say without sounding completely disrespectful.

"Are you getting ready for class right now?"

"No, mom. I don't have class until 12:30 today. I got really lucky and didn't have to take 8:00 classes this semester because of my dual enrollment credits. It's really early; is everything okay?"

"Are you in your room by yourself?"

"Yes, I am. Sharon is in class right now. I was sleeping until the phone rang," I lied.

"Mom, what is wrong? I know that you are not an early morning person, so what is wrong? What happened?"

"Nyla, Baby."

Now I know something is wrong. She has not called me baby since the beginning of Olivia's senior year of high school. What in the world could be wrong?

She continued, "Your father is… "

Before she could finish the words, I was screaming.

"My father. Mom, my father is what? My father is what?"

"Nyla, there was an accident on the docks, and your father… well the doctors said he didn't suffer at all. He died instantly."

116

All the blood drained from my body at that moment. I was numb, speechless, heartbroken, and choked out of any words that could possibly come out of my mouth.

My dad was a Gladiator. There is no way he is gone.

She began to sob on the phone, and I could not move for what felt like days upon weeks upon months. Every second that I sat there, the pain intensified, and I could not contain myself. I wept. I wept for my Dad, Olivia, and Baby Dylan. I wept for my sisters and brothers, but I could not weep with or for my mother. I just hung up the phone without saying another word.

Chapter 16- Gladiator Gone

I was on autopilot. *This three-day weekend could not have come at a better time*, I thought as I made my way to my classes.

I had made the decision to go to class for the next two days, and would go home on Wednesday after my once a week 12:30 class. No one suspected that I was going crazy on the inside; I was holding it together.

That Wednesday afternoon, Sharon and I drove to Miami in almost complete silence. The closer we approached the Miami Turnpike exit that led to my house, the more real it became to me.

My father…my amazing father is dead.

I began to sob in the car. I had not wept or said a word about my father since I hung up with my mother that Monday she gave me the news.

When Sharon came home from class that day, I could tell she already knew what happened by her puffy eyes and look of concern for me. All of my siblings loved her, so any of them could have called or texted her to tell her the news.

I couldn't do it. I just continued to get dressed for class. She walked over to me to give me a hug, but I stopped her.

"Sharon, please don't. I just need to get to class. You know I can't be late for this class."

She looked completely baffled. "You're actually going to go to class. How?"

"Easy," I replied in a very serious tone. "My dad would kill me if he knew I missed class for any reason. You know how he is about me and you definitely know how he is about school. I have to make him proud. He's counting on me, and I don't want to let him down."

She continued to look at me in amazement. She was speechless.

I was finishing the last of my makeup and said, "Bye, girl. See you later."

As I walked out the door, I could see her mouth open in awe, baffled.

Until that car ride, she had not seen me break down about my father. I was so determined to be strong like Olivia would have been, so I kept my emotions bottled up inside. I suppose they had to come out at some point and this isolated car ride where I had nothing but my thoughts to keep me company made me an easy target for a break down.

Sharon pulled over and just held me. I did not object or stop her this time.

I just cried and cried and cried and cried some more. She just held me and cried too.

"My dad, Sharon! My dad is gone. Sharon, my dad is gone." I managed to sob out before I could no longer speak, choking off my shortness of breath, honestly hoping that I was dying so that I could be with the people that I loved so dearly. It wasn't so, and as Sharon was trying to calm me down, I gathered myself and just drained all the water from my body with my tears.

As I briefly closed my eyes, I continued to weep. It's so hard to believe he is really gone. I remember in the fifth grade for my advance English class, we had to write a paper about one person who we called a hero. Without hesitation, I chose my Dad. I title the paper, "My dad: My Hero". I can still recite the paper by heart because later, I made it into a poem.

My Dad my hero tall and strong: My Dad my hero how can he last so long.

A man born to a mother and father with his early life torn apart;

By drugs, alcohol, and violence that threatened to stop his own heart.

My Dad and hero at a young life knew who he was not going to be:

He would not be a hustler, or abuser, or an alcoholic wino under a tree.

He wouldn't be like his brother Elijah or Norman or Butch

He would be an honest man and bless everyone his life would touch.

My Dad and hero he didn't have it easy in his life,

But he went to school graduate and took up a trade to quickly settle family strife.

He met the love of his existence at the corner store

buying a honeybun

When she looked up at him, he couldn't move, walk, or

run.

My Dad let her take his heart and married her as soon

as he could,

He became a husband then father and employee to lay a

strong foundation like a real man should.

My father is my hero because he never stops trying and

loving me best.

He is a strong man a real man and anybody will have to

pass my Daddy Hero test.

As I opened my eyes, I continued to feel the warm tears flow down my face. Sharon just sat there and waited. She let me cry and daydream because no words could come out- she just waited. What a friend. What an amazing friend.

Chapter 17- The Horror Show

Sharon really is an amazing friend, just like you are, so I have to apologize to you Friend. As you are going through this journey with me, I promised to be completely honest with you, so let me tell you what really happened that day in my room when I found out that the love of my life, my father, my dad, my hero died.

As I sat there, I really tried to remember in my head all the techniques Dr. Newton tried to teach me. Dr. Newton tried so hard to show me techniques to help me when I began to feel anxious and depressed and hyper active all at the same time after Baby Dylan's death and then it just got worse after Olivia died her senior year of high school. Yes friend Olivia my older sister and best friend died. It was awful, but I'm not ready to talk about it yet.

That day in my dorm room I could feel all the emotions rushing through me and at me all at once. I tried to remember the words of affirmation and the breathing exercises, but all I could see was my brother, sister and now father's dead faces. I closed my eyes and refocused, and all I could see were dead bloody faces. Daddy, then Liv, then my Baby Dyll Pickle. Then there they were again dead in coffins- cold and unemotional.

All I could do was scream. Just scream and scream and scream.

I turned the music up as loud as I could without getting a noise violation. Why the hell did I care? I turned that damn music up to maximum high capacity.

Blue there! Yellow there! Put a little red on it! Then a dash of black! Yeah I like it! These walls needed a little color. Sandwich time! A little mayo here and a little marinara sauce there! Sprinkle some bacon bits on top of some pickles and then a little mascara here and some lipstick there. Jungle gym! Yeah jungle gym! Come on Baby Dyll Pickle! Come on! Let's play dress-up Liv. Let's make a sandwich collage Baby Dyll Pickle. Daddy, I promise we'll clean it all up. It's art! Look, Daddy! Art.

I heard the door open, but I was in playtime with my sister and making a lunch collage with my brother Baby Dylan. *Daddy! Come have a macho sandwich with us. Come eat, come eat.*

"Umm, Hi Ny." Sharon's eyes stretched wide as she looked around in complete disbelief, but then she did something that brought me back to reality.

"Ny. It's 12:00. You're going to be super late for class if you don't go get dressed."

I realized at that moment that I was completely nude with a mess on my hands, and actually all over me. Shit was everywhere.

I said, "Yeah, Sharon. You're right, I should" And that was that.

I gathered my necessities, went into the bathroom, got dressed and headed out the door for class without looking back.

As Sharon witnessed my meltdown in the middle of our room, she didn't say a word about it, and when I came from class later that day the room was completely spotless.

She never said a word about it from that day to this one, and I hope you won't either. You know I trust you friend. I'm telling you some really heavy secrets. But you can trust me. I'm not crazy. I promise I'm not.

Chapter 18- Beautiful Ceremony

Friday. The day before my Dad's funeral was here, and I was in complete auto pilot mode.

Funeral arrangements with program completed...check.

Cream outfits for funeral services for my siblings and me...check.

Friday wake and viewing arrangements
complete…check.
Announcement posted in the Miami Times
check.
Notification to all relatives and friends…check.
Program and poem completed for
services…check. Wait no- that's a half check.

I knew that my dad would want to hear one of my
poems. I had written him one every Father's Day and
birthday. It was our tradition. He never wanted a gift. He
said my precious gift of poetry was priceless, and he was
always honored that I would write one especially for him.
My Dad was my hero, so writing for him was my honor. He
made it easy to have new material every year. What better
time than this to write about my hero, and so I did.

Heroes are made, built, cultivated and primed.
My Father is the greatest hero to me- one that
made him divine.
I stand here before you all, remembering so
many times and so many ways
that my Hero saved our lives and loved us as if
he were our slave.

125

They say the greatest and only commandment is
to love God and thy neighbor,
So my Dad possessed a gift that made his
existence about others to love and labor.
He is a giant, a great man of sorts: he is a
believer and he never dropped the torch.
My father had a wife and nine children he
adorned
He made us all feel fearless without negativity
and never did he scorn.
Once I was talking to him about life and the
subject of boys
He said, "Nyla, no one will ever love you like
your Daddy but never be one of his toys.
As serious as I love you, your man will do the
same.
He won't use you or abuse you, but he will give
you his last name."
I remember when I stood before you, reading
for Olivia, talking about the pain.
I can't even begin to talk about this pain now
because I know myself, I won't regain.
My Father, my hero, the love of my life has been
taken from us in peace and no strife.

*I don't know when I will see him again or when
the void will ever go away.
I just know that he blessed us on this earth for
fifty years and could no longer stay.
My Dad, my believer, and my friend is gone
now, and I must hold onto him within.
He loved me like a daughter, sister, homie, and
best friend.
Many will say it will be okay or he's with God
now or I'm sorry for you loss
So my Father will forever be loved and his life
touched others with a priceless cost.
He was a kind man, a strong giant and
committed warrior innate,
so look for him to claim victory when standing
at Heaven's gate.
My Dad never had a load of things to say, but
what he said, he said it well.
Therefore, let this day celebrate him and how
much he loved because we all have amazing
stories to tell.
Do your crying for our Father, Friend, Loved
one, and Warrior Innate*

But a great man is at rest now and that is what
we should celebrate!

As I finished reading it to myself, I prayed that when I read this at his funeral, I read it with pride and not grief.

> *"Lord give me the strength and courage to speak these words and bless the listeners of my words. May they feel special and inspired by my gift of poetry. Thank you and Amen."*

*

As we prepared our home for company after the viewing, I was on level ten with bossiness, and no one dared test me. They all knew better- even my older brother Joshua. The law allowed Josh to be home with us to bury our father, but he had to go back directly after services. There were armed guards there to make sure that happened.

As I was barking out my next order to my siblings, Rashad walked through the door. *Good- another laborer that could give some help*, I thought as I motioned to him to come fast and get started on the next task. We had not talked much at all since I got to Tallahassee and definitely not since I found out about his hoeing ass.

I guess you already know my genius plan of revenge on Rashad was put on hold. We definitely had more pressing matters than getting his cheating ass back. He bought himself some time because from the time I reached my home in Miami until today, he has been there. I'm sure one of my siblings or even mother called him to tell him about my father earlier in the week because I damn sure didn't. In any case, he was there waiting for me. I looked at him with pure disgust, but he just assumed I was stricken with pain over my father. What a dumbass! He didn't care about what order I barked at him; he just complied. He did whatever I needed and I was more than happy to tell him what was in demand and had to be done.

*

The entire weekend was absolutely beautiful. My father is a great man and the weekend demonstrated that to magnifying levels. Things had been so busy that it was impossible to concentrate on anyone other than my Father. He was the center of the weekend, so I was happy being busy for him. He deserved it.

It's so hard to believe that he is really gone. I remember in the fifth grade for my advance English class, we had to write a paper about one person who we called a hero. Without hesitation, I chose my Dad. I titled the paper, "My Dad: My Hero." I can still recite the paper by hard because I made it into a poem. It's where I got the inspiration to write the other poem.

My Dad my hero tall and strong: My Dad my hero how
can he last so long.
A man born to a mother and father with his early life
torn apart;
By drugs, alcohol, and violence that threatened to stop
his own heart.
My Dad and hero at a young life knew who he was not
going to be:
He knew he would not be a hustler, or an abuser, or an
alcoholic or buried six feet.
He knew he would love others and have a lot of kids to
care for
My Dad, my hero and friend would be the one to
cherish and more.

As I sat in the living room, Rashad packed up the car, so Sharon and I could get on the road to drive back to Tallahassee. I hugged all of my siblings, including Joshua, as if this was our last time ever seeing each other. I wanted them all to know how much I loved them and how hard life would be without either of them on this earth. However, my embrace with my mother was certainly different. It was full of emotions- love, disdain, joy, pain, and finally forgiveness. We could both feel the healing in that embrace and it was magical. We cried in that embrace, we choked up in that embrace, but we didn't let go until it was finished. Until all the begrudging and pain was gone, we held on. We held on until we felt better, until we felt whole, until we felt like we were a part of one another and until the love we once had was restored.

That moment in our family history was magical. Deliverance was there. Healing was there. Joy was there. Change was there. Victory was there. A brighter future was there. We all felt it including the bystanders. Sharon, Rashad, Kendra, and my Dad's crew who stayed over to help us clean up and see me back off to college. Everyone was touched and that magical moment gave me all the strength that I needed to go back to school and finish strong.

My mother and I released our embrace free, changed, renewed and whole. Looking directly into my eyes, my mother said, "Nyla, I apologize for it all. I never meant to..." I stopped her with another embrace.

"Mom, as Dad would always say, it is finished and all is well."

We kissed and expressed our love for one another, and as I looked at the twenty plus people looking and crying tears of joy around us, my sister, Sadey, the youngest in the room and definitely most energetic screams, "Group Hug!" I promise her cheerleading and gymnastics spirit was always a blessing in our home. We all did one huge hug and my father's best friend led us in a prayer that made the house rock and the angels above blow peace on all of us.

Our drive back to Tallahassee was so much better than our drive down to Miami. Sharon and I talked about the entire weekend, but mostly we discussed the miracle that occurred in my house.

I was so mad at God before, but I have no issues with him now. My Dad was still a giant in his death; he brought his family back together. Let's hope it lasts long.

CHAPTER 19- The End of SEMESTER ONE

With only two more days in the semester, I am happy about my successful academic career and pleased with the lessons I have learned this semester. The death of my father is still something that I deal with every day. Rashad still has no clue that I know about his cheating ass.

*

Let me pause right here because I have to tell you, Friend, that I did sneak down to Miami after my father's funeral weekend to see him. During that two-day visit, I gained access to all his stuff. I now know his school email accounts and login for classes, all the new credit cards he acquired, and his new bank account information that was tied to his school money. Oh my, the things I could and would do. While I was there, I convinced him to take me shopping and give me three months' worth of bill money totaling about a grand. This was just the beginning. He was going down.

*

Now back to my end of the semester summary. Sharon is my true best homie and the best roommate I could have asked for. Jeffrey and I, though not an official couple, were getting closer and closer every day. I was going to miss him over Christmas break.

Since I returned to Tallahassee from burying my father, he had been right there for me. We talked all the time. He would call me throughout the day, and we would talk while at work, sometimes during our study breaks. There were a few times I was almost kicked out the library for being on the phone with him. He sent me a gift almost every other week. Last week, it was a Candy Care package. The week of homecoming it was a First Timer FSU Homecoming Gift Basket. Another time, it was a School Supplies Care Package. He was so damn thoughtful. I wasn't sure why we weren't a couple but the love we felt for one another was real. I had fallen in love with him at orientation, but would never admit it out loud. Since he declared his love for me that night at his place during the FSU/UM game, he was in hot pursuit for my heart. I was still reluctant and didn't want to start anything with him while being so bitter against Rashad. Jeffrey was too good for me to do that and just as I was breaking out one of my many daydreams about Jeffrey, the phone rings.

When I saw that is was Jeffrey calling me this early Saturday morning, I was excited and answered the phone with a huge smile on my face.

134

"Hi, there. Good morning to you," I smiled as I greeted him on the other line.

"Hello?"

My smile was destroyed and heart crushed as I heard the girl's voice on the other line.

CHAPTER 20- Christmas Break in Sunny Florida

After the phone conversation with the chick who claimed to be Jeffrey's high school sweetheart, I decided to go to Sharon's house for the Christmas break. I couldn't bear to go home and see Rashad. I would take every bit of my anger out on him. I really couldn't and didn't want to see my mother. My siblings were safe and so I was good not seeing them either. So, Tampa, here I come. It was my first trip to the West coast of Florida and I was super excited to see how it shaped up compared to Miami during the holiday season. Boy, was I impressed.

Sharon took me everywhere.

We had breakfast at First Watch every day that we could get up in time for breakfast. That restaurant was delicious. I was hooked on the seasonal pumpkin cake breakfast and the pumpkin pie oatmeal. I would go back and forth with my ordering. One day, I had the pumpkin cakes and the next day, I had the oatmeal. When we were going to the beach, I would just have my Kale Tonic juice from the juice bar. It was a delicious mix with just Kale, Fuji apples, cucumbers and lemon. It was perfect for beach time. Then we would head to a few different places for lunch depending on what we were doing.

Some of our usual lunch spots included Bahama Breeze or Kojak's House of Ribs or Oystercatchers in the Hyatt Hotel on the beach. We loved to go to Simply Good for the soul food. Well, let me say that *I* loved to go to Simply Good. There was this sexy azz guy that worked in the kitchen. I would make it a point to smile back there on every visit. He would sometimes come to the front during our visit so I could see all of him. You know guys do the same things girls do for attention and to be seen, and I sure was looking that peanut butter brown sugar man. Yes, I was.

Our lunch choices completely depended on our tongue, mood, and outfit. When we wanted good seafood, we would frequent Bahama Breeze because their food was consistently good. Sharon knew a lot of the servers and bartenders because her family did a lot of business with them, so we would get great hookups. We would order

Virgin Pina Coladas or Daiquiris and bring a special potion to mix in. Though the staff loved us, we were discrete with that part. Didn't need them blowing up our spot or more importantly telling her Dad what we were up to during our lunch breaks.

We went to Busch Gardens and then hung out in Ybor City. We said we wanted to have every minute of our break packed with no room for free time and forget sleep. We probably slept two to three hours max every night. We hit every club in Tampa and the surrounding areas. Since it was the holidays and schools were out, it was a new world of dudes to meet, and I surely took advantage. Even though we went out with money in our pockets, there were so many nights that we came home with that money and more. I guess everybody was in the spirit of giving, and so thank you sir, we gladly accepted all gifts.

Since we were just a short car ride from Orlando, we planned to go to all the After Christmas sales there. We went to the Premium Outlets first, but they weren't open yet, so we headed over to the Mall at Millennia. As we walked through, we talked, laughed, people watched and flirted our asses off. Sharon was definitely more flirtatious than I was at that time. We were always seeing who would be the boldest and come up with the best pickup lines, so

137

today we had a bet going to see who could pick up the most men and get the most phone numbers. Hell, we figured guys did it all the time, so why couldn't we?

We walked in and out of some of our favorite stores like Lacoste, Macys, Abercrombie, Forever 21, Coach, and my absolute favorite, Aldo Shoes. There were sales occurring everywhere. The kiosks in the middle of the mall halls even had great sales. Two for one here and seventy-five percent off there and buy one, get two free here. It was like we had just hit the retail lottery. And Aldo was no different. This shoe store was known for having the most stylish shoes with some of the best sales that made them all affordable. Now let me say Friend, if you have not been to Aldo Shoes, first slap yourself and then get up right now or as soon as they open and get there!

Aldo is by far one of my favorite shoe stores to date. You can find some of the most popular styled pumps there and one of my favorite styles, ankle boots, in which I had on today. My Keshaa Red Ankle Boots bring sizzle to any outfit I put on, so today I was giving everybody fever with the peep toe and a form fitting jean mid-thigh dress that accentuated my small waist and flaring hips with my red accessories, cute hoop earrings and flashy button that lit up to say *Santa's Best Helper*. I thought, *Why not? Tis the*

138

season to be jolly, so we walked into Aldo with nothing but shoes on our minds. As I walked into my shoe heaven, I got a glimpse of myself in their mirror. Oh my Aldo, this is yet another reason why I love you.

Their mirrors always make me feel good about myself. They seem to always accentuate all the positives about people. As Sharon walked by, I had to admire us both. As I thought it, she said it.

"Damn, Ny. You are giving that dress the business! Ms. Fashionista!"

I smiled. "It takes one to know one, girl!

Sharon always said that she dreamed to have a shape like mine, but I really loved her shape as well. She was taller than I standing at 5'11 while I was 5'3 and a half. I always told people, 'Don't forget the half.' I would sometimes roundup to 5'4, especially when I was with Rashad because he was 6'4. It used to sound cute to say we were a foot apart. He used to love to pick me up and bring me to his eye length. He always told me how pretty I was and he loved to compliment my physique. I had the same shape since I was twelve and it caused everyone in my family, especially the men, to be overly protective of me. I had a true Coca-Cola shape. Men would always call me brick house, but at twelve, I was so self-conscience of my shape. I didn't like all of that attention. Today, though, I knew that I looked good and felt so confident. I was in my own world. You know, *everybody* should have those days.

And then from the back of the store, he came… Dammit, man because he was… the sexiest damn man alive!

"Excuse me, Idris, can you help me please?" I asked knowing that wasn't his name, but 'Jesus Rodriguez' it should have been.

He smiled and said, "I'm Carrington, and I'd be delighted to serve you."

Yes, baby come serve me, I thought as I smiled and showed him a black matted style thigh high boot I had been holding for ten minutes as I perused the store searching for my next shoe best friend.

"Do you have these in an eight and a half?"

"I believe we do. Let me check, and I will be right back."

"Yes sir; make sure you come right back Idris…I mean Carrington." He smiled and kept his eyes on me until he had to focus on his path ahead of him to the back stockroom.

Sharon was peeping the scene and just burst out laughing.

140

"Girl, you win! You win! I cannot believe you called that damn man Idris. You are a pro with this pick up line shit!"

"Ha! Thanks girl! I've learned from the best!"

We just kept chuckling and I smiled as I remembered my smooth ass uncles and their game. Miami men certainly kept you on your toes, and my favorite uncle always told me to never be taken- always take. My sister, Olivia, used to always say, "We know what to do and how to do it, but Ny, we have to use our 'powers' for good and not evil." She was always so positive and optimistic. I would always listen to her every word. The men in our lives were always telling us how to know when guys were trying to play us. They would sit us down and talk to us all the time. That's why I can't believe I fell for Rashad's bullshit and then turned around and let Jeffrey pull the damn wool over my head, too. Ugh! Just the thought makes me want to slap somebody, but as soon as Idris walked around that corner, I was back in Chocolate Heaven.

This man was a beautifully painted picture; an absolute perfect work of art. There must have been a law against being that damn fine. Shit there had to be a law. Hell, I thought Rashad was the finest man I had met, and Jeffrey was certainly the most alluring, but Idris Carrington was a complete defiance to all that I had known when it came to sexy, fine, alluring, mouth dropping, statue of perfection.

Idris Carrington had to be about six three, dark chocolate colored skin, with beautiful locs that flowed to the middle of his back. He had the body and hair of the other love of my life, Demond "Bob" Sanders, safety for the Indianapolis Colts, but possessed everything else that Idris Elba embodied. He was absolutely delicious. He glided across the floor as if he knew he was the only man worth looking at in the entire store. He wasn't cocky though. I hate cocky arrogant men. He was just so damn confident that he needed no introduction. He had so much swag and sex appeal. Man, I had to stop staring. It was becoming obvious and I couldn't let him see me fantasizing about him completely naked. He was just so gosh darn sexy, just dripping sexy. It was bleeding through his pores all over anyone who was in his presence. He wore tan tailored slacks with a bold rustic brown, tan, and deep orange sweater and a crisp white dress shirt under it with nice copper bronze cufflinks to top it off. He had on some two-toned tan and brown hard bottom shoes from Aldo, of course, with brown Kenneth Cole frame glasses. This man was sexual- someone that you would see on a magazine cover. He did not have to do anything but stand there and you would have thoughts of ecstasy. He could get you there without laying a hand on you. *Oh my word, this might be the one to get it!* I thought as he assumed the position on one knee in front of me to unveil my requested shoe selection.

"Here you are; I was able to find your size." And there was that smile again. You know that smile that just exudes confidence but not arrogance, sexiness but not freakish, classy but not snooty. This man, and yes he was damn sure a man, was iconic. He deserved his own TV show. I would have titled it, "How to Get a Woman Without Saying a Damn Word!"

"Thank you so much Carrington."

"You're welcome, Miss," as he extended his handshake to me where I gladly jumped at the opportunity to touch him.

"Nyla. I'm Nyla Howard."

"It's a pleasure to serve you, Miss Nyla Howard. Please let me know how you like your boots. These are an excellent choice for you."

As he walked away and disappeared to the back, I could not help but stare and fantasize about his sexy ass all over me. *Good Lawd, Nyla. You need to give up that kitty soon and to him before you pop!* My thoughts were interrupted by Sharon's presence.

"Umm girl- are you going to try on the boots or not? I know he's fine as hell, but you can't wear him on your feet."

"Girl, but I can damn sure wear him everywhere else. Shit, Sharon do you see how fine that man is? How old do you think he is? I'm thinking he's probably twenty-eight or twenty-nine.

"Girl, I'd probably give him twenty-nine."

As I slipped the boots on, I fell in love all over again. These thigh high boots with the stiletto heel were giving my height life and more. I stood at 5'10- okay almost- with these boots on. I walked around the store checking for comfort or at least making sure they fit, and I could get from the car to the table in them.

I was so mesmerized by the new loves on my feet that I didn't even see anyone around me.

"Oh, I'm sorry. I didn't see you," I said as I realized that I bumped into another woman who appeared to be looking around as well. I guess.

She gave me a weird look and just proceeded out of the store.

Okay. Don't know what that was about, I thought, but who cared. These boots were amazing.

As I continued my walk around past the register at the front of the store, Mr. Idris came from the back once again to see me strutting my young sexiness all over that store.

"Absolutely beautiful," he said, as if he could not hold his comments any longer. "You are absolutely beautiful, and those boots say so as well."

I damned near tripped over his words and into his arms. He was so damn smooth.

"Thank you." We just stared at one another.

"Please forgive me for staring, but I truly cannot help it."

"You are forgiven, and you can stare at me for as long as you want, Idris."

He smiled, and I had to remind myself, *that's right, Nyla. You've got game too. Don't let him be the only one running it.*

"If I may, Miss Howard, would you like to go to dinner with me tonight if you are not busy?"

"Well, I'm here for the holiday visiting my friend and her family."

"Oh okay," he interrupted, and to avoid me saying
no, he said, "May I take you and your
Friend? I'll take you your friend and her entire family to
dinner if I can see you again."

He gestured to Sharon, and said, "So dinner
tonight?" As if she was the decision maker in our
relationship.

Sharon jumped in and answered before I could-
"Yes. Yes you may; just the two of us, though."

He smiled at her, and then looked at me and handed
me his card and a pen. May I have your phone number,
please so that I can call you to discuss the details for
tonight?"

"I can just text you my number so you'll have it."

"Thank you, but I'd rather have a written account of
my first encounter with you. I don't want to forget anything
about you Miss Nyla Howard."

'Oh, shit this man is different. Hell, yeah you can
have my number, my name, hell my social security number
if you keep talking like this, 'I thought to myself.

He handed me another one of his cards and said,
"I'll call you very soon and you can call me anytime.
Please call me anytime, Miss Nyla."

Aww, shit, I thought. Every time he said my name I got moist.

Well, Nyla. Get it in gear. It's on to the next one.

*

That day was full of fun. We had lunch at the California Pizza Kitchen and then decided to go to Macy's and look for an outfit to wear for our dinner with Carrington later on that night. As we left Macy's, I said, "Sharon, let's go to David Yurman. There is this bracelet that I absolutely love, and I want to admire it."

I didn't tell Sharon about my father's will and life insurance money. I just told her that I wanted to look at the bracelet with her, but I planned on buying it as soon as the funds appeared in my account. My mother and I had a huge massive blow up a week after my father's death about the money he left us, so I didn't want to share with anyone else what was left to me for that reason. It was crazy how people act over money. My mother definitely did not deserve what my father left her, but I guess it wasn't enough. I just kept thinking that you can't teach an old dog new tricks. My mother was a piece of work and not in a good way, but as I got closer to Yurman, my thoughts of Nancy Francine Howard drifted away like ocean waves.

My David Yurman classic bracelet with 14K gold balls and accents with the DY large oval link bracelet to accompany it was all I needed to get my mind back into a healthy happy place. That bracelet and its trusted linked friend were going to be my only expensive gift set I bought for myself, and then I would save the rest to help me through the end of my school career which would be at least seven more years because I had plans to go to law school after I earned my Bachelor's degree.

If I budgeted correctly, I would have enough money for my Bachelor's degree, law school, and a down payment on my first house with a nest egg start up fund for my law firm that I would open within five years of earning my Juris Doctorate.

*

As we walked into David Yurman, I felt important. Greetings from the sales associates and offers to assist us in any way just made me feel like a millionaire. I smiled and acted like I was not impressed but I was definitely beaming inside. These people knew how to get the sale. We browsed and look from case-to-case. My phone rang as I spotted my future bracelet in its temporary holding place.

"Hello?" I said as I smiled at my bracelet smiling back at me.

"Hello, Miss Nyla Howard."

"Carrington, Hi. Long time no see." We both chuckled, as we knew it had been less than three hours since we saw one another. "How are you doing?"

"I'm wonderful, Miss Nyla. Missing you, honestly."

Oh yes sir, tell me all that I want to hear. Lay it on thick I like it. Those were my thoughts, but my words to him were, "Oh, that is so sweet."

"I wanted to call you as soon as I could to let you know my potential plans for us for tonight. I made reservations at The Capital Grille for three at 8:00 tonight and then booked us three tickets to the Improv to see Kevin Hart and thought we could hit Blue Martini and such after that. What do you think? Are you free and up to it?"

"I sure am. Excuse me, *we* sure are Carrington. We are in David Yurman right now and were headed back to Sharon's parents' house after this, so that gives us great time."

"Oh, David Yurman is a great store. They have high quality pieces. Send me a picture of what you're thinking of buying. I'd love to see your taste."

"I sure will Carrington, and I look forward to seeing you tonight."

"Oh and please text me Sharon's parents address.

I'll send a car for you all."

What the heck, I thought, as I said goodbye. A car?

What the hell did he really do for a living?

Chapter 17: Building My Stable

For the last five days of our break, we spent it with Carrington. He wined and dined us at all the nicest places in Tampa and Orlando. This man was so much fun. He was extremely intelligent and had earned his Bachelor's in Business and Masters of Business Administration from Stanford University. He had no children and from what I could tell was not married nor did he have a girlfriend. He was great company and outstanding conversationalist. He knew how to hold his liquor and he had an affinity for good cigars. Carrington was a class act, and there were several times that I was so relieved that Sharon was with us because he would have taken my virginity several times after a long day of fun, food, and conversation. But the night before we left to go back to Tallahassee, Carrington Devoe almost made me fall in complete love with him.

*

Sharon and I had been at the beach all day. We decided to spend our last day "funning" in the sun. Carrington called us early that morning and invited us to an evening we would not forget, so we thought we would get up, stop by Fresh Watch for our special juice and go have a beach day with enough time to come back home and rest for the evening festivities. He told us that we didn't need to worry about what to put on. He had that covered, so we were free to have a stress free day at the beach.

The day was shaping up to be just beautiful. The men were plentiful on the illustrious sands of Clearwater Beach. I wasn't really interested though, but I still entertained a few of them with some conversation and empty promises to call them later. The sun was our best friend and all these beach body men made me happy to be a woman. Goodness! So much to look at and I've tried to see them all.

As I took another look around, I observe that this girl is staring at me.

"Sharon do you know her?"

"Who?" Sharon replied, as she automatically looked around aggressively.

"Sharon, don't look. Gosh you're going to make it obvious."

"So I don't care. If she's staring, I *need* to make it obvious."

"The girl over to your left with the curly long hair
and black bathing suit with the silver cover-up,"
I said quickly.

"Oh no, girl. I don't know her, but the only thing cute on her is her hair. Damn, there ought to be a law about a black woman having no ass."

"Sharon, you are a nut. Girl you're crazy," I chuckled.

*

Ok, friends. Y'all know me, and know I always meet a few prospects, so there were a couple of dudes that were noteworthy: Sexy Six-Packed Pecan Tan Jonathan and Bobby Brown look alike Samuel. Who knows why the hell I let Bobby approach me, but I did and didn't regret it. That fool was hilarious. He had a great sense of humor and confidence that was seductive. He just knew he could get anyone on that beach that day, so I ignored his azz most of the day. He would walk back and forth past me. I would shift my eyes, so we never made eye contact. He finally just came by and fell dramatically in front of me. I continued to ignore his ass.

"Oh my goodness! Ouch! I think I pulled something. Are there any concerned ladies around?"

Yep, he's faking, I thought, so I kept ignoring him.

He limped-crawled closer to me as if he wasn't close enough for me to hear or see him and kept up the dramatics.

"Oh, I'm in so much pain. Oh my goodness! Miss can you help me, please. I think I broke, sprung, and twisted something."

I just stared at him, and burst out laughing. Sharon and I both did at the same time. He was so dramatic and his face looked like your family dog, Fluffy, begging for affection at your feet. He just kept staring with his silly smile and gorgeous eyes to compliment his full lips. I was such a sucker for men with beautiful eyes and nice lips. I always felt like you could tell a lot about a man through his eyes and lips.

"Miss, why must I go through so much to get your attention? I have walked past you over twenty plus times and you never looked my way. Goodness. I had to drop and damn near roll around in this sand to get your attention. You must have a man?" He looked at me matter of fact, and I just smiled.

153

He muttered, "Dammit! The exotic ones are always taken."

Exotic! Oh my thanks! I definitely chose my bikini with care. It accentuated all of my features and gave no room for error. It was bright neon colors like yellow and pinks with red undertones and a beautifully black base. The top was slim and covered just enough of my breast to be legal while the bottom hit all the most important places. This bikini was my new favorite and one of my best purchases from our after Christmas sale. I loved it and my shades were true hater blockers. I only wore them when I saw a male nuisance approaching like "Bobby."

Sharon exclaimed, "Dude she's not taken; she's just not interested in you. Gosh why can't you take the twenty plus hints she sent you?"

That seemed to fuel his persistent fire.

"Well kind madam friend to the girl of my dreams, I have been hypnotized by Miss Taken, excuse me, Miss Uninterested, and I just need to be let out of this trance. Only she can do it." He stared at me like Fluffy again.

"Boy please! You are too funny. You have so much game." He really did look like Bobby Brown and now he surely was acting like him.

154

"I'd play whatever game you want me to if that results in your name and number."

"I knew you weren't Fluffy."

I don't know who Fluffy is, but I can be whoever you want me to be for that name and number.

"Ok Bobby. My name is Sharon," I said.

"Bitch, what? I don't think so!" Sharon screeched out followed by a huge belly laugh.

Ugh, I thought. *How embarrassing. She could have gone along with it.*

Sharon and I chuckled as I said, "Okay, Mr. Bobby..."I'm Lala." Lala had a cute ring to it, so I would use that as my alias from now on.

"That's better," Sharon said as she laughed and got up to go walk into the beach water to set her beautifully developing tan.

*

Let me just pause right here and say that many may think we shouldn't tan, but who gives a care about what anyone else thinks. We loved to tan. It made all of our melanin pop! We had a complete plan to it. This rich skin tone was a process! Since I care so much about you friend, I'm going to give it to you for free, but you can't share it with anyone. I might consider selling this on EBay!

155

Successful Melanin Tanning 101

First, you need to plan for the right swimwear. It has to be something that will leave minimal tan lines. If you are tanning multiple days in a row, use the swimsuit that leaves the smallest lines first. That is crucial, so wear a string bikini on the first day.

Next, is the very important day- The morning of- you must check for sunrise time. Plan to be out on the beach an hour later. Morning sun is perfect - not too hot so you can get comfortable for a morning nap on the beach. Don't get to the beach later than 10 a.m.; you won't find a good location and the sun will be BLAZING by then. Also, before you get to the beach, Shower! Forego your regular everyday lotion and slather on the sunscreen. SPF 50 or higher - preferably sports strength. Once you get to the beach scope out your prime location - far enough away from the pedestrian walk paths but close enough to the shoreline. The MOST IMPORTANT location piece is an area with a wide enough circumference to rotate your lounge chair or towel to remain directly under the sun! Oh, yes, you should get a lounge chair. You'll be less likely to get sand kicked or blown on you as people walk by and/or the wind blows. Don't get too close to the shoreline; you don't want to get wet from the waves.

When you find your location - spray on your BRONZER! This is the small SPF stuff - like 5 or 10. It's usually a spray or oil and very greasy. This is what we call the "Rotisserie Spray." Spray and turn. Spray and turn. Just like the Rotisserie chicken in the deli.

When you are ready to grace the beach goers with your beautiful body - lay on your back first. Leave the sunglasses off- no raccoon or patchy eyes! Untie your top and tuck the strings into the boob covering part of your suit. The goal is no halter tan lines. Fall asleep for about an hour, hour and a half. If you bring reading materials, be sure they won't block your sun exposure.

After 90 minutes - take a walk into the water. Saltwater works well with your Rotisserie Spray to bronze the skin. After your water walk, reapply your sunscreen. All ova yo' baaaaawwwdy! Now, reapply your Rotisserie Spray. Lay on your stomach. Untie your top in the back and let the straps fall. You can wear your sunglasses now. Take another nap. When you wake up - remember that your top is not tied!!! Don't wanna give the people too much (unless you're on the Rainbow end of South Beach - The Kids are topless friendly).

Re-tie your top. Go for a dip in the ocean. Check tan progress. At this point, its lunchtime, which essentially means DRINKS!! Grab something quick and easy to eat. Bring your drinks back with you. Bucket drinks are the best – easy, refillable, and usually slushy which means easily drinkable. After eating, reapply sunscreen and Rotisserie Spray. Lay on your back. Untie top and tuck straps into boob part. Fall asleep again. Wake up - take a dip. Take a walk to let melanin challenged people go gaga over your complexion (and wondering why YOU want to tan and take their good sunrays). Reapply sunscreen and Rotisserie Spray. Lay on stomach and untie straps in the front of the top and bottom of your bikini top. Take another nap or read. By this time it's about 3 to 4 p.m., depending on how long your naps were. Now you can "play" on the beach because your work is done. You should reapply sunscreen and Rotisserie Spray every 2-3 hours to minimize sunburn. For the rest of the weekend, wear clothing and colors that accentuate your hard work!!

Oh wait! Music! You need music, which means you'll have headphones and that will mean possible lines. When listening with headphones while tanning, place the headphones in your ears from BEHIND. You should be lying on the cord. This eliminates those tan lines.

Bobby proceeded to come closer.

"Well lady, Lala. I'm Sir Samuel of the Tampa Bay region of Florida."

This guy was funny. It was cute, but I didn't let him know, though.

"Well, Sir Samuel of the Tampa Bay region of Florida, why are you so concerned with getting my attention? It was certainly apparent that your day has been consumed with meeting ladies.

"Oh, so you did notice me! Damn girl you're good.

I didn't think you knew I was alive."

"Bobby. I'm sorry, Samuel. *Damn Nyla!* I laughed at myself. *You have got to stop uncovering your nicknames for these dudes.* "What can I do for you?"

"Well, first you can give me your phone number, let me take you out and maybe have my baby after we get married in a few days."

"Oh, Jesus Rodriguez," I said as I let out an explosive laugh.

Now, Friend; if you're not from sunny South Florida, you may not have heard 'Jesus Rodriguez 'before. It is like saying oh Lord, but so you're not saying the Lord's name in vain, you add the Rodriguez to the end.

159

I kept chuckling as I thought *I definitely need this man in my stable.* He was hilarious. You always need a variety.

I could hear my uncle's words of wisdom to my brother, Joshua, ringing in my ear. Uncle Nelson never knew I was eavesdropping, but I was and really hard. I heard all of the trademark secrets to getting women and keeping them, so as I reflected on the past six months of my freshman life, I began to realize what I needed to do. I was well on my way to getting my stable of thoroughbreds up and running for my affection and their lives with me, of course.

As I smiled to myself and acknowledged that he was a good addition to my stable, I gave him what he came for- my number and a semi-honest promise that I would let him take me out sometime soon. He walked away at just the right time because Mr. Pecan Tan walked up with a couple of bottles of ice cold Aquafina Water for Sharon and I.

"See you later, Sir Samuel."

"Hi there! These are for the two of you."

"Aww thank you, Jonathan. *Mr. Pecan Tan, I said to myself.* How nice of you. I was just thinking that I could use some water." Jonathan was a cool brother we met as we walked onto the beach. He carried our bags and helped us find a good spot. He was nice.

It was so funny though. I could not believe how fast these men were coming from every direction. It was like they were standing in line just waiting for the one in front of me to walk away. Jonathan seemed to be sweet though. Definitely not my regular type, but I would converse with him for a little while.

As Sharon approached from her dip in the water, a young man stopped her, and they talked for what appeared to be an eternity.

Damn, I thought. He must be interesting. Sharon doesn't entertain anyone for more than a minute or two at the most. She was more of a heartbreaker than I was. She was a cold smooth operator. So that dude must have had some strong quick game for Sharon to stand there and talk to him. She even seemed enthused. Wow what a switch.

Jonathan took Sharon's distraction as a perfect time to occupy my time and space with his cute self.

"Seems that your girl is busy. You want some
company?"

"Sure, Jonathan sit down. Let's chat."

At that very moment, my phone rang and it was Mr. Idris.

"Jonathan, please excuse me for one second. I need to take this call." Without moving my body, I just repositioned my phone to have a semi- private conversation with Carrington.

"Hello?"

"Hi, beautiful. How are you enjoying your fun in the sun?"

"I'm excellent and loving this sun. It is a beautiful serene day out here."

"I just wanted to call and say I miss you and can't wait to see you soon."

"Aww," I said trying to be sweet but nondescript so Mr. Pecan Tan wouldn't pick up on my flirtatious tone.

"If it's okay with you all, I wanted to send a car for you both from the beach at about four. This will give you all time to get here and ready for our evening."

Oh friend, I am so sorry. I forgot to tell you. Mr. Carrington sent a car for us this morning and it took us everywhere we wanted to go and waited at every spot. Then as the driver dropped us off at the beach he told us to enjoy our day and see you both soon. It was so hard to think of anyone else besides Carrington, but I had to. I couldn't get my feelings caught up in another man right now- especially with my hate and anger still brewing for Rashad and Jeffrey.

Chapter 21: Beach Pickup by Rich

One of his drivers, Rich, picked us up promptly at four in front of the beachfront restaurant at Clearwater Beach. Rich was always nice to us since our first ride with him on the first day we met Carrington, so we were happy to see him again when he pulled up.

"Hi, Rich! It's so good to see you again. We thought Chuck was picking us up?" I asked.

"Oh, yes he was supposed to, but the boss has him taking care of something else, so here I am."

"That is cool Rich," Sharon said while she smiled.

I think that Sharon was really feeling Rich, but she was trying to play hard to get, which was very rare for Sharon.

We slid into the comfortable leather back seats of this sweet and sexy Mercedes E-class 320 and dosed off to sleep. I had a beautiful dream that this black on black nicely tinted car of perfection was mine, and Carrington, my husband, had a matching red one that he drove around himself. But he always provided me with a driver for my

Benz. Oh what a life I would live to be in this man's world. He was so infatuated with me, and I surely drooled internally enough for me to be in lust for him. He just made it so easy to want him and that night was no different.

As Rich pulled up to Carrington's driveway, there he stood. My own personal Idris Elba waiting for me to arrive to him. Yes, he really liked Sharon, and he knew we were a package deal, but he was always waiting anxiously for me. It felt good to be longed for like that. That shit was sexy as hell. Jeffrey always had that longing in his eyes for me as well, but I guess it was all fake. I had to pinch myself before I got out the car to get my head back in the game. *Forget Jeffrey, Ny and thank God he is gone for the spring semester on his co-op for his Engineering major. You won't have to see him the entire semester.*

Carrington didn't wait for Rich to do his job; he came to the car and opened our door and smiled so full and sexy as he saw me step out first.

"My goodness, woman, you are beautiful in anything that touches your body."

I still had on my two-piece string bikini that was bright and full of bold illustrious neon pinks and blues and yellows with gorgeous black accents at just the right places. I never felt the need to wear a cover up, but I did respect his interior and spread a towel on the seat when we first got in at the beach. He was ever so impressed with my curves in my bikini.

"Nyla. Oh my. I'm speechless. You look so delectable. May I please kiss the woman of my every fantasy?"

"Oh, Carrington .You really know how to spread all of your charm on me." I gave him a tight hug where I could feel his Hercules rise to command and attention in his pants, but I didn't release or pull back from our embrace. I wanted him to know that I was ready for everything his Hercules had to offer me. Hell, Carrington deserved everything I was going to bless him with that night. He deserved all of me. He had paid enough attention, money, and care to get my special delivery. I wanted, no fuck that, I needed him to know that I was ready.

I hadn't told him that I was still a virgin, and I didn't feel the need to share that with him at all. I had enough fantasies in my head to have "devirginitized" myself years ago. I decided after Jeffrey that I was going to start fulfilling all of my fantasies. I know Dr. Newton would probably object to me taking these actions, but I didn't care at all. I was ready to quench every sexual thirst I had. I was ready to have all my needs met starting with Carrington.

Through those linen pants, I could feel that he was blessed and bountifully endowed with the best of all worlds. *Thank you Jesus Rodriguez for the honor of being touched by such a penis. I appreciate the opportunity to get to know him sooner than later.*

He pulled me just far enough from him to look into my eyes.

What is with these men and looking in my damn eyes? Goodness.

"Nyla, I apologize but I can't help it. Every time I'm near you I get so excited from head to toe. Every part of my body desires to be near yours."

I just kissed him with the perfect balance of passion and lust, and pulled him back close to me. He loved it. Yes, another hooked thoroughbred.

Sharon and her rude ass interrupted a perfectly good foreplay session with the infamous "Uhh Umm." I ignored her, but of course she did it again in rapid fire.

"Uhhmmmm! Uhhh Ummm! Ummmm! Uhh! Uhhh!"

As I pulled away from Carrington, I just looked back at her as I walked into his front-all glass-with gold-framed doors and rolled my eyes. As he led us to his uniquely designed bar lounge, I just admired every inch of his multi-million dollar home along the way; he had an open floor plan. I loved open floor plans. You could see the entire main floor once you entered the front door.

He truly spared no expense and it constantly made me wonder what this twenty-nine year old man did for a living. This had to be drug money, and if he kept sticking to his story about being an IT guru who created some app and website and sold them for millions of dollars, I was going to scream. This is the type of home that belonged to a fifty-five year old mogul but instead it was in the hands of this young chocolate hunk of a man named Idris... Carrington.

Yes friend, I said it twenty-nine, and you already know I'm nineteen, but the way I see it, women are much more mature than men; therefore, he is really only about two to three years older than I am in maturity. It all balances out and since men my own age are whores. I might as well check out older men. Hell, at least they have more money and time to show me new experiences, but back to his house. Don't get sidetracked, friend.

He must have had an interior designer. His home was the perfect blend on classic and contemporary art deco. As you walked into his front doors, which were sparkling white glass that shimmered one's reflection, allowed him to see out but visitors couldn't see in, he had an all-white formal living room area, which sat off to the left. When you stepped down into that living room area, it was magnificently decorated with plush uniquely designed chairs and sectional pieces that fit perfectly to the next piece. Just exquisite.

His bar had everything you wanted in life from any alcohol and wine fantasy. The man was a superstar in my eyes, but I didn't let him know how much he intrigued me. He loved chasing me, so I always played his ladylike innocent well-endowed princess. I would be anything he wanted me to be. I knew his pockets were overflowing, so let us play.

He had Prosecco and St. Germain and a beautiful fruit and cheese tray waiting for us.

"Ladies. May I offer you a drink?"

Without hesitation, Sharon and I said yes in unison.

"Thank you, Carrington. You shouldn't have?" I asked.

"Baby, I had to. You just take my breath away."

168

I blushed and smiled. He really was a sweet guy.

We drank and ate and hydrated ourselves with the ice-cold water that he had decorated with lemon and pineapple floating inside a glass picture with a nozzle large enough to provide the perfect flow of this delicious water. Carrington was out of a movie. He did all the right things and said all the best words to make me want to drop down and bow at his feet, but I didn't. Instead, I complimented him on his taste in wines as I saw that his kitchen and bar areas had wines decoratively placed from all over the world.

We headed to the other side of his home where one of his three guest rooms was located with its own bathroom and lounging area. When we walked in the room, I almost staggered at the sights- racks of dresses and heels of all kinds on shelves with accessories that sparkled and flashed bright rays of colorful beams around the room. We had stepped into a shopper's paradise. One thing Carrington knew is what he liked to see a woman in, and I was A-Okay with that about him. Everything he had selected would fit my size seven to eight frame. It was sometimes a challenge for me to find bottoms that fit me perfectly because of the voluptuousness of my hips, so my preference was always a dress.

On these racks in this room, he took the liberty of selecting dresses of all lengths, colors and styles. As I walked around the room though, I could see that he sprinkled in some mini and pencil skirts as well as some nicely tailored shorts and pants that would paint "irresistible" all over my body.

He knew I was impressed; shit I couldn't hide it and I had to tell him so with a huge hug and deep lustful kiss.

"Baby: thank you so much. I knew you said you had everything covered, but I was not expecting this at all. You are such a wonderful man."

Sharon had to give him his props. They exchange their nods of approval and sealed it with some dap and sibling like embrace.

He said, "I'll step out and let you all decide and get dressed. We have dinner reservations at 7:00 p.m., so that gives you all about an hour and a half to get dressed before we have to leave for the evening. Please make yourselves at home and anything you want is yours to have."

As he shut the door, Sharon and I screamed with our mouths but made sure no sound came out. We jumped around in a circle like little schoolgirls on the playground.

"Can you believe this shit?" we both said at the same time.

"Girl, this man is unbelievable. I am giving him some tonight, Sharon. I mean that."

"Child, I don't blame you. He deserves it."

As I walked into the lounge area right before the bathroom, another huge smile blared my face.

"Sharon, girl. Come here." We had drinks chilled in sterling silver pails and a fruit and cheese spread that was more impressive than the one at his bar.

In the bathroom, I felt like a little girl about to play dress up. He had purchased every lipstick and eye shadow that could possibly match any of the outfits. He paid damn good attention to me because he had selected my foundation and brand to perfection.

As we finished the last of our makeup, we heard a gentle knock at the door.

"Ladies it's about time to go. I will meet you all at the front door."

As we made our way to the front door, I could see that Carrington certainly took time to shop for himself as well. He was in a perfectly painted on tailored Ralph Lauren blue suit with a sparkling white collared dress shirt with custom made cufflinks with his initials and a symbol that looked like an eye.

As he stood there and marveled at my beauty, I could see both of his hands were occupied- one with a gorgeous impeccably selected bouquet of roses and the other a neatly wrapped box.

"Nyla, you look stunning. You never seem to stop taking my breath away."

That was my plan, baby, so mission accomplished. I knew that the all-white Ralph Lauren form fitting knee length tube dress with rose gold stiletto heels would take his breath away, so that is what I put on. With a beautiful diamond necklace set and flawless diamond tennis bracelet to match, I wanted him drooling for me at first site.

"These are for you," he said, still star struck by my beauty.

"Carrington, you are doing too much, and I thank you for it. These roses are beautiful. May I leave them here? I don't want them to be harmed in anyway."

"Please open this. I believe it will suit your outfit perfectly." As I opened the box, I screamed. It was my David Yurman bracelet set that I told him about on the first day we met. He bought me my bracelet set!

"Oh my goodness, Carrington. Poppa- thank you so much." As I embraced him with the sexiest kiss he had ever received from me, I knew he was the one to have my precious jewels tonight. He was getting all of me tonight.

Chapter 22- Bat Shit Crazy

We experienced VIP treatment from the front door to the back. It appeared that everyone knew this man from the staff to the other party goers. One thing is for sure was that he was only focused on me. Women were coming from left and right front and back, but he kept his focus on me.

"Hi Carrington, "What's up tonight?"

"Hey there, lady! Drinks on me. Enjoy yourself."

"Thanks, Boo. I will see you later."

He didn't respond but just looked at me to see if I was bothered.

Hell, no I wasn't bothered. I was that bitch tonight, so I didn't care anything about yesterday's bitches and their need to regain their spots. "Good riddance twitches, good riddance!" I chuckled out loud to myself at that one.

*

Carrington wasn't a dancer, but Sharon and I definitely were. Well, let me say that Sharon danced to any song and all night long. I was a selection dancer. If my songs came on, I was up and shaking my stuff like an award winning dancer. If you were lucky and they came on back to back, you were in for a show, a real treat. I love *Vanity 6- Nasty Girl. She's a Brickhouse* was my theme song, but if you played *Trick Daddy's- Can't Fuck with the South* and in that order, you might just clear the dance floor, let me have it, and watch me move. Once you applauded my performance, the melodious sounds of *Frankie Beverly featuring Maze- Before I Let Go* would bring us all back together on the dance floor. I loved me some Frankie Beverly featuring Maze.

Carrington loved to watch me dance, so I think he had the DJ play my songs in order and that's all I needed. I could always get Carrington to join me on the dance floor for this song. It was the perfect two step song for him, so as he made his way to me on the dance floor, there was one guy who must have been new to this area because he didn't get the *Nyla is off limits tonight* memo.

As I waited for Carrington, still dancing to *Before I let Go*, I could see this clueless silly man approaching in my peripheral. As he spoke the words, "Excuse me," and reached to tap me on my shoulder, two guys out of nowhere in discreetly intervened. One of Carrington's people stepped in between us and the other escorted him to the left, and there was Carrington in front of me ready to dance. He appeared to not see anything, but the entire scene was hard to miss. *Hmm* I thought; *this man has some serious connections.*

The night moved on beautifully. Carrington actually danced a lot longer with me than usual. I felt like he truly designed this DJ's playlist. It was a perfect combination of shake it fast to Groove Theory to let's make a baby tonight music.

There were so many eyes on us. Spectators all over watching to see what we did next. *Goodness*, I thought. *There she is again. Who in the hell is that girl?* The same girl from the beach is here tonight and staring, yet again. I know I don't know her, but maybe she knows me.

As a song came to a close, I was so hype, but I asked Carrington to excuse me for a second so that I could go and talk to the girl.

Hell, let me just go ask her if I know her, I thought. She might be one of my distant relatives or something, but as I walked towards her, she disappeared. It was really weird, but who the hell cares. I was having a blast.

As the night was nearing an end, Carrington said he had to talk to the manager of the club for a second and had Rich escort us to the car. We walked to the car waiting for us outside with ease. It was like the seas were parted and we had a clear path from the dance floor to the back seats of the car. As we sat comfortably waiting for Carrington, Sharon saw one of her high school sweethearts, Kareem, from out the window. I saw her inside the club with him and realized that was the same guy she was talking to at the beach earlier and that she couldn't stop talking about at Carrington's house earlier today. She stepped out to talk to him and about five minutes later, she was asking permission to be excused for the evening. As if she needed my permission to get her some high school sweetheart love, I chuckled. I already knew she would be gone with Mr. High School at some time during our break by their chemistry at the beach earlier.

"Love you girl. Call me when you're headed back my way. Be safe girl. Have fun!"

We hugged our usual embrace, and she was gone in the wind with her old/new Bae.

176

As Carrington approached the car, I could tell something was wrong. He looked ungathered.

"Honey, are you okay?"

"Yes."

Oh my. A one-word answer is all that he gave me. I definitely knew then that something was wrong.

"Home, Rich," and that was all he said for the ride
   back to his house.

No questions about where Sharon was or explanation about why we were headed back to his house early. Just "Home, Rich," and his face out the window. It felt like I was riding with a complete stranger who had kidnapped me and I was on the way to my death. That was the creepiest ride ever, but nothing was scarier than when we were finally alone in his home.

Rich said goodbye to us and walked to the cottage that he lived in on Carrington's property. I could tell he was accustomed to Carrington's behavior because he didn't make any sudden moves and just gestured to me to be calm. As Carrington opened the door and allowed me in first, he sighed and began to cry as he closed the door behind him. He dropped to his knees like a person who just received news that someone close to them had died and continued to weep.

"Poppa." I sat in front of him and held him close to me. "Poppa, honey what's wrong?"

He just cried, and I was really terrified. I didn't know what to do. *Shit,* I thought. *I'm really living on the edge. If this man snatches my ass up, I probably deserved it. This living on the edge shit might not have been worth it.*

He began beating his own ass. I mean slapping himself, punching himself in the face, calling himself dumb ass, weak ass, stupid ass. Oh my gosh, friend. I was no longer afraid for me. Hell, I was afraid for him. He was beating the shit out of himself. Now this, I could handle. I thrive in dysfunctional crazy mess thanks to my family, so I got my thoughts together and jumped into "Nyla helping her crazy ass brother Joshua" mode.

"Carrington! Carrington! Carrington! Stop! Stop NOW!" I knew he wouldn't hurt me, so I moved closer to him and that made him stop. See my twin, Josh, used to have episodes like this and the only one he wouldn't hit is Olivia. She knew exactly what to do, and he would let her calm him down. Since Liv was no longer with us, we just all fucking prayed that he wouldn't have any episodes because we couldn't calm him down.

With Carrington, I was his Liv. I knew that he would not hurt me. He would have done it by now, so I took off the gorgeous dress he bought me and began to clean him up. As I talked softly and slowly to him, he began to come to his own senses. I poured the water that I had been drinking in the car on my dress and continued to clean all the blood off of him. He let me. Then the shit happened- just like Joshua's crazy ass, Carrington jumped up like he didn't just beat the crap out of himself, and screamed, "Ok Ny, let's eat! What would you like to eat? I have everything and I'm cooking."

"Baby, I think I'd like some pancakes."

"Pancakes coming right up," and just like that it was over, for now.

Oh, hell no, is all I could think- this man is bat shit crazy, but at least I know this type of crazy. Josh has adequately prepared me, but DAMMIT! There goes my 'giving up my virginity' fantasy. For now, it was up in smoke, but he was still a contender.

Chapter 23—Back in School for Spring Semester

I was on the Dean's list from the fall and headed back on her list again this Spring semester. I had a 4.0 from fall semester. Though it was my first semester in college, I was not surprise by my great grades. I worked hard for that 4.0. No...I worked my ass off for that 4.0. I had no choice but to ace all classes. I had to make my father proud. He was always concerned about my academics. He would say, "Education first and everything else will fall into place." I used that to get through the chaos of last semester. I had to just smile as I thought about him. My dad kept me from doing a lot of damage to a lot of men. *Come on back, Nyla*, I said to myself as I thought about the low lives from the fall: Rashad and Jeffrey. Those two gave me some great material for my poetry book. The first poem I write, *Dark and Lovely,* was just one of many that gave me clarity and strength to move on.

Dark and lovely, short and tall, make all your women call
and fall
Feed their hunger, tell them lies, seal with kisses and
enchanted eyes.

Shade them foggy, give them fear, and make their worst
dreams reappear.
Send them off cold without shelter- rearrange their lives
into endless welter.
Never let them see the worth that pulls them higher beyond
this earth.
That moment when the clutch is lost and all control is
shattered and tossed.
The line they'll draw to get about; to run around aimlessly
trying to get out.

Those two will get theirs soon enough, I thought as I laid across my dorm bed staring at the ceiling. Sharon came in and broke my silence which was a good thing because I was headed down a winding road of mischief.

*

As we sat there preparing for our "last weekend of freedom" gathering in our dorm, I could not contain my excitement for this upcoming semester. There were so many things to look forward to: New Orleans for Fat Tuesday in February- Mardi Gras here we come- and Jamaica for Spring Break. I was ready to take Nyla and the Posse international. Then we definitely had to be ready for Memorial Day Weekend on South Beach in May. It was too bad that Freaknik in Atlanta wasn't still around. I heard

181

so much about it when I was in high school, but I think we had enough to be a part of to keep us occupied. Goodness knows I needed it, especially with the loss of my Dad and my anger for Rashad and now Jeffrey. Anyway, let me not think about it.

At the Tennessee Street Waffle House after the BSU Ball last semester, my girls and I had a full planning committee meeting for our spring semester as we ate some All Americans to soak up the alcohol we had during the course of the evening. Of course, the actual ball was a dry affair, but we certainly had creative ways to enjoy ourselves with some special mixtures in undisclosed places, so the night was great and our spring semester planning productivity was off to an awesome start.

We knew the cold months of January and February would be over soon, and we would be beach body ready. I had certainly gained the freshman fifteen, but Carrington said all my weight was in all the right places. But my girls and I seemed to be in the same shape, so we made a pact to lose what we gained by spring break. That meant I had fifteen or so pounds to lose in two months. I could do that with a lot of working out and starvation. We were all excited- especially since we all got along so good. When Kendra came up for FAMU homecoming in the Fall, she and Sharon hit it off beautifully, and Sharon's friend, Joy, was super cool. The four of us were a true squad, so we planned our "last night of freedom" gathering for just the four of us to chill before school started the next day. Kendra didn't start school for another week, so she was more than happy to join us in Tallahassee, especially since she had been gone to South Carolina for the entire Christmas break with her family.

*

The four of us had so much fun that Friday night before the start of spring semester. We laughed, cried, drank and plotted. Friend, we discovered that we all had dudes in Tallahassee and surrounding areas who had broken a piece of our hearts. That night we planned our attacks on all of them bastards. Sharon's was Kareem, Kendra's was Barry, and Joy's was Al. You already know who mine were- Rashad and Jeffrey. We were going to get them all back and in different ways. All we knew was that it would be Biblical how we were going to crucified them. They would think twice the next time they messed with another woman's or man's heart, for that matter.

Yes, believe it or not, it had been revealed that not only were some of them jokers messing around on us with women but some of them had men, too. That made me even

183

madder because not only were you lying about cheating, but you were just cheating with the entire human race. One thing I hated more than anything in the world was a liar. I don't care who you chose to date or be with in your life, but lying to me about anything was the worse you could do to any relationship you had with me. All of these dudes made me sick, and they deserved everything coming to them. Yes, they certainly did.

"Umm, why wait y'all? Let's get 'em tonight." Kendra said and just like that we all agreed in unison with, "I'm down," and that is how *Payback Friday* commenced.

*

It was on that night that we had five unsuspecting targets that were going to feel some of our pain and the thunder of our wrath. They had no idea what was headed their way. One would be sparked, and another keyed, while another spray-painted and some cyber-attacks on the ones we couldn't get to physically.

"Let the games begin!" I shouted. "But, I have to use the bathroom first." I laughed and head to our room to grab my journal on the way to our bathroom.

As I sat there on the best bowl throne ever, I had to talk to my dad for a little bit.

Dear Daddy, I wrote.

I miss you. I wish I had the words to tell you how much. If you were here, you would have the words to say to talk me down to make me refocus. If you were here, you would love on me and make me forget all the bad stuff that has happened. If you were here, you would hold my hand and remind me of my worth and tell me not to worry about any of them because they're all fools. If you were here, I would believe that men are still good and I just fell for a bad one, but you're not and so I must do what I feel is best to do.

Love,

Nyla

I jumped up feeling energized and justified.

As the rest of them finished getting dressed and gathered all the supplies we needed, I pulled out my laptop and went to work on the cyber-attack on Rashad. I wanted him to suffer the worse for what he did to me and it was time to start taking action. First, deplete all money from his bank account. Men can be so dumb. I had all of his information: social security number, passwords, date of birth; correct spelling of his name and perfect imitation of his signature. I had all of his accounts, a book of his checks, and a debit card for his account. Dumbass. If he

185

was going to cheat on me he should have at least changed his passwords. I knew everything, so it was so easy to maneuver through his life and destroy it in ways I saw fit because in my eyes he was the start of the end.

Rashad was the reason why I fell head over heels in love with Jeffrey. He was the reason why I was in pure lust for Carrington and the lifestyle he led. Rashad was the reason why I had a strong male stable, full of men who were all willing to suit and satisfy my every need and desire. If I could mesh all of them together they would make the perfect man, so dammit it is his fault. He is the reason why a good girl has gone completely bad. Yes, I tried to reel myself back in and even thought of calling Dr. Newton. Lord knows it had been years since I talked to her, but I didn't want to hear her psychoanalyze me. So, oh well. I'll just work this out in revenge.

"Bam! Done!" I shouted as I hit the button to wipe his account clean. I was in complete go mode now. "Let's go girls. We got shit to wreck," I said as I grabbed Kendra's keys and headed out the door.

Chapter 24: Wreck It

We jumped out the car dressed in all black with spray paint, spark plugs and sharp edge screwdrivers. In less than sixty seconds, Jeffrey had "The Nyla Bell Effect:" a shattered front view and back view (thank you, spark plugs), "Bitch" engraved on both sides, and spray paint across the hood, "Never say never."

Jeffery decided that he wanted to play games with my emotions. No, we never said that we were exclusive. No, we never said that we were in a relationship, but he should have known that all the nights I spent with him were about something. It had to mean something. Since it didn't mean anything to him, Jeffrey deserved his new car detail. We were back in the car and onto our next target in less than two minutes.

We jumped out at the next deserving victim, Al, and felt really good because Joy had a tracker set on his phone and it led us to another girl's house. Al and Joy had been high school sweethearts and had moved to Tallahassee together. They lived in the same complex but separate apartments. He told her over winter break that he wanted to marry her, but needed some time apart. That didn't make any sense to any of us, but she felt that he had been cheating. Well, her suspicions were correct because as we looked into the windows of the townhouse where his car was parked in front, we could see him in there snuggled up with some trick. Yes, let's get his ass. He got the same detail job as Jeffrey, with some bonuses. We put sugar in his tank and flattened all his tires. "The Joy Effect" was the best of the night.

We wanted to be smart about the next three, so we decided to plan a Payback Friday trip to Miami for Rashad and Kendra's low life Barry. We would have to get Sharon's piece of shit that I really thought was a nice guy, Kareem, on another Payback Friday. We would have to go back to Tampa for that fool, or we could tell Carrington what he did and leave it to him to give Kareem all he deserved. Heck yeah; that is what we will do. Carrington loved Sharon and so when he hears about how Kareem did her wrong shortly after we left Tampa, he'll get his men to give him everything he deserves and more.

"Girls! What a great night! This is going to be an awesome semester!" Sharon screamed as we finalized our payback plans in Kendra's car heading back to our dorm.

We all laughed and agreed.

*

"No! No! Stop! Don't!" I jumped up out of my
sleep to an empty dorm room. Sharon, Kendra, and Joy
decided to go and get some late night food from the Waffle
House, but I decided to stay in and try to sleep. It had been
a long time since I had any of *those* dreams. I never wanted
to talk about any of that stuff. It was nobody's business.
My therapist used to try and get me to talk in our sessions
about my feelings and about Olivia and my uncles and my
childhood, but I wouldn't. How was I supposed to tell her
about what was going on with me at the age of five and
then six and then seven and then nine and then Baby Dylan
and then Olivia and then and then and then?

The thoughts flooded my mind and I burst into
uncontrollable tears- streaming hot burning blistering tears
that felt like my heart would pound out of my chest.
Seriously friend, how was I supposed to disclose all of the
hidden secrets that nobody knew- that nobody would dare
share. I couldn't tell her about Uncle Elijah or Uncle
Norman who caught Uncle Elijah. I'm sure someone told
her all about us, my siblings and I, so why the hell did I
need to talk about it? What would that do for me?

I had grown numb, strong, resilient, and dangerous. Dr. Newton seemed a little passive and naïve like I used to be, so she surely wasn't ready for all of the history that I had, all of the memories that I buried and blacked out of my mind and life. No, there was no need to talk about any of that shit, so though Dr. Newton was really nice, I just couldn't share any of that. So let's refocus my energy.

Yes, let's focus on that bastard who has my mind in a world wind. Rashad. Rashad River Jones. He is my public enemy number one. Decision made; it is all Rashad's fault, and the cyber-attack on his bank account was just phase one.

Sleep tight Nyla. Sleep tight.

Chapter 25- Men, Men, & More Men

It was official; the weekend before school in Tallahassee was full of events and had gotten off to an exciting start. Our Payback Friday attack was a huge success, and the next couple of days were jam-packed with events. There was an Indoor pool party of magnificent proportions at The Gathering. Nobody cared that it was cold outside because all those sexy bodies made it sizzling in and around that pool. Then there was a spades tournament party being held at one of Sharon's friend's apartment clubhouse. We had a few house parties in which we had to make appearances, the BW3 club, and the Let Out at the Moon on Saturday night. Since we weren't old enough to get in, hanging out in the parking lot across the street gave us a lot of actions with the men coming out of there. We would dress up like we just came out and when they asked where we were all night, we would say, "Oh, by the bar, or on the dance floor or chilling by the DJ booth." We would say anything not to get found out. I loved me some older men, so I needed them to believe that I was on their level.

This particular weekend was magical for me. I met so many people and came in contact with some old friends as well. I was trying to snag any man walking around to intensify my stable. I didn't want to be at a loss or longing for attention. I needed men, men, and more men in my life to fill the blank moments, to fill the parts of my mind and heart that still had Jeffrey entangled in it. I couldn't shake my thoughts of him. I was so puzzled by how everything ended. Carrington was a great filler of space and though he was bat shit crazy, I enjoyed his company because he kept me completely occupied.

*

This indoor pool party was shaping up to be a blast. As I stood there looking just as sexy as I wanted to daydream about all the man pieces I acquired, I hear, "Excuse me. Excuse me are you Nyla?"

"Yes, I am," as I turned around to see an unfamiliar yet female face standing before me. I knew I didn't know her, but she looked like someone I had seen before.

"I'm Jessie."

"Jessie," I repeated looking puzzled.

"Yes, Jessie. Jeff's girlfriend."

I stood there for a long while looking completely lost in space. When I put on my two piece Jamaican colored bikini this morning with my matching flip flops and bangle earrings in sure anticipation of the largest conglomerate of fine ass college men with shirts off and six packs, I had no idea I would be meeting any girlfriends, let alone Jeffrey Donovan's girlfriend.

"Okay, yes. Jessie. Hi."

"Well, the last time we spoke our conversation was cut short and I thought we could talk for a little bit today."

Ummm, what the hell is this girl thinking? Talk? What the hell do we have to talk about? This is a pool party with the finest men in college here at the same time. There is more than enough men for me to turn around four times and still see a different set of abs that would make you want to slap anybody's momma. What the hell is wrong with this girl?

"Jessie, listen. I heard everything you said on the phone during our one and only conversation, and we truly do not have to talk about anything else. Now if you will excuse me, I truly have some men to meet. Take care."

As I walked away, her mouth motioned as if she had much more to say, but as far as I was concerned she could say it to the fucking air. I was out and ready to mingle. It didn't hit me until I was on my fifth set of heart dropping abs and that this girl's eyes followed me around the entire damn party. She could not stop staring at me. I didn't know why she was so latched on to me- especially since she had Jeffrey, so she said.

What the hell was her problem? She was making some of my girls mad with her strange behavior, but I didn't care. I was all over that party with major goals in mind. I had a calculation that I wanted to solve. How many six packs could I take home with me tonight? Let's see, John yes you can go; Fred, no you had to stay. Fabien, hell yeah you could go and stay all night, and Brett you could stay the whole weekend if you like. I was on a mission. I needed the V before my name to no longer represent virgin. I had some very good prospects to make that happen and happen soon. I had to go to Student Ambassador training the next day, but I was determined to make this the last night of my virgin life. Tomorrow, I wanted to walk in there smiling from my "loss."

"Hello. Your cup looks empty. Can I get you something to drink?"

My eyes were on the pool at the time trying to decide if I would at least sit and get my feet wet. To my pleasant surprise, I looked to my left to see a wonder in the land of wonders. My goodness! Can this day have gotten any better? The men I met up to this point certainly were noteworthy but this man was book worthy. Damn man can I author your story? I screamed inside.

"Actually, I am fine, thank you. I was actually probably about to leave in a little bit so I need not drink any more lemonade." I smiled as he chuckled.

"Oh, wow. You don't drink or just not today?"

"No, I'm not drinking today. I have a long weekend of training tomorrow and Sunday, so I need to be completely coherent and attentive to get through it."

"What type of training?"

"Student Ambassador for Florida State."

"That sounds important. I'm Daniel Perry."

"Nice to meet you, Daniel. I am Nyla. Yes, I believe it is important."

"I believe anything you are involved in is important. You are absolutely beautiful on the outside, and it seems like you are on the inside as well."

"Oh, my Daniel. Such strong words for someone you just met. Thank you for the compliment. I feel compelled to do great things now." I smiled flirtatiously. He certainly took all the bait. He didn't look like the gullible type. He was an intellectual. I could tell by his word choice and mannerisms. Yes this would be a great addition to my current stable.

"Miss Nyla, I am a great judge of character; not to mention I have watched you since you entered this gathering. You are breathtaking, and your air is alluring."

"Daniel, you truly are a breath of fresh air. Are you from here?"

"No, I am actually from Houston, Texas. This is my first year in graduate school at FSU."

"Oh well, that is rather impressive, Daniel. This is my first year here at FSU as well. Undergraduate of course."

"Oh, really, Nyla. You're a freshman?"

"Yes sir." I smiled confidently and proud.

"You truly are an amazing woman, Nyla."

"Again, Daniel; you truly have the sweetest compliments."

"What are you majoring in, Nyla?"

"Currently, English. My plans are law school after this."

"Law school. Attorney Nyla..."

"Howard," I said proudly.

"Oh okay; introducing the beautiful and highly intelligent Attorney Nyla Howard."

He shook his head confidently and with mere admiration, he smiled. "I like it. I like the sound of it."

We stood there envisioning me answering to such a power title and smiled at one another with what could have been interpreted as love by any onlooker. Our gazes into one another's eyes seemed so heated and intense that neither of us recognized when Sharon's crazy ass walked up.

"Ugg. Umm, excuse me Nyla. We are about to leave. Are you able to walk?"

"Very funny Sharon. Of course I can."

"Daniel, this is my very crazy and inappropriate roommate and best friend Sharon. Sharon, this is Daniel Perry a new friend and first year graduate student at FSU."

"Oh okay, then Mr. Grad School. Nice to meet you. I must get my friend out of here, so she can get ready for tomorrow. She's Miss FSU Ambassador. Maybe she can be your student ambassador?"

"Oh my gosh Sharon! You are crazy! Give me a second! I'll be right there."

He smiled and blushed all at the same time. Sharon truly had a knack for doing that to people.

"It was a pleasure to meet you, Sharon. I do hope to see you again."

"It appears that you will with the way my roomie is acting."

"Bye, Sharon! I'll be right there!" I pushed her away so that she could move along swiftly before she said anything else to completely embarrass me.

"Umm, Daniel?"

He stopped my explanation with sweet laugh.

"It's all good Nyla. Your friend is hilarious. I certainly miss my friends back home."

"Oh yes, you did come all the way from Texas. Have you been able to meet anyone to hang out with here yet?"

"No, not yet. It is different from undergrad. It was much easier to meet people then. Now everyone is so focused on passing these classes that they don't even look up or around to have any fun."

"Well, Sharon might be right. I may need to be your Student Ambassador."

"If you're serious, I would love that. You seem to be a cool person to be around."

"I want to believe that I am Daniel." We both smiled again with that intense gaze that got us called out about a few minutes ago by Sharon.

As he continued to stare into my soul, he spoke so softly.

"Nyla. May I please have your phone number, so that I can call you and set up our Student Ambassador tour?"

"Of course you can, Daniel from Houston, Texas in our illustrious FSU Higher Education graduate program."

He smiled a beautifully immense smile that spread his gorgeously perfect white teeth across his sexy luscious lips. As I continued to stare at him, he blushed in my presence; I took his phone from his hands, texted him, then called as well as left a voicemail on my phone from his.

"Good afternoon, Nyla. This message is from Daniel, the gorgeous graduate student you are standing in front of at this very moment. He is interested in you being his personal FSU Student Ambassador because he thinks that you are beautifully alluring with a sweet presence. Please give him a call at...I look at him to say his number... he begins 346... I repeat... 346... he continues... 297, and I smile and say 297 while he finishes 0909... as I end 0909... Please give him a call at your very earliest convenience. He can't wait to see you again."

As I hang up and pass him back his phone, he just continues to smile as he enjoys watching me work his phone as if it were mine.

"Nyla, you are funny. I do look forward to seeing you again very soon."

He gently pulls me close to him and kisses me on my cheek while his arm embraces the small of my back.

Damn this man is smooth as hell. I am growing to love these Southern men. They are so smooth.

"See you later, Nyla. Enjoy your training."
"Thank you, Daniel."

As I turn to walk away, I can feel his gaze and certainly as I turn back for one last wave goodbye, Daniel is standing there attentively as if he can't break the trance that I put him in.

I wave and smile...

As I meet my friends who are waiting for me at the complex entrance, I chuckled. Men are such gorgeously simple puzzles that I love to work for my benefit.

Chapter 26- Relapse & Payback

Towards the end of the fall semester, at Dean Chen's recommendation, I applied and was accepted into the illustrious world of FSU Student Ambassadors. It was such a great honor and I was so proud of myself. Dr. Newton would have said this was a win for me. I was feeling so confident because my Student Ambassador group was full of people I didn't know and boys I was in no way attracted to. When I walked into the first day of training, I thought, *Great. No distractions*. Everyone was super cool in my new world of Ambassadorship. They were from different walks of life and majoring in a range of fields from Aerospace Engineering to Underwater Basket Weaving. These were some really cool people. We kept in contact over the break via group messaging, email, text and some phone calls, so I was genuinely happy to see all of them.

As I walked into the University Center, heading for the designated training area, before I saw him I could hear him, and before I could hear him, I could smell him, and before I could smell him I could feel his presence. I began to shiver with so many different emotions, and I felt like every step was taking me deeper and deeper into quick sand until I finally couldn't move.

Jeffery.

He saw me and it was like our souls and spirits merged into one.

"Nyla, hi I'm so happy to see you! I've been calling you all break. Please talk to me. What did I do? I knew you would be here, and I just wanted to talk to you before I left for California. Please talk to me. This has been the worst two and a half weeks of my life. I know I should have told you about her, but we were over. She just didn't want to accept it. I was at my parents' house and she came over claiming to want to see them. She took my phone and called you. Nyla please, please just talk to me. I would never do anything to hurt you, please." He just rambled on and on. I just looked at him with no words.

"Nyla, I love you. I love you. I love you like I have never loved anyone before. I am sorry about everything. I would never hurt you. Please…"

After what appeared to be an eternity of me staring at him, I fell into his arms and let him embrace me while I embraced him right back. I loved this man. I couldn't help it.

*

Friend, I know you're probably disappointed in me, but I couldn't help it. Have you never been in love before? I loved this man!

I knew that Jeffrey was telling me the truth about Jessie. That explained why she was behaving so strange at the pool party. She was desperate to reclaim something that she had lost, and it appears that she lost him because he fell for me. Knowing this information, how could I hate him? How could I not love him? He had been through so much because of me.

Before my father passed, he called my room once and Jeffrey answered the phone. Oh boy why did he do that?

"Hello, Nyla and Sharon's room," Jeffery answered authoritatively.

"Yes, and who is this?"

"This is Jeffrey, sir" he said.

"Well, Jeffrey, son why would you be answering my daughter and her roommate's phone? Did you send her some tuition money that I don't know about? Did you pay for the phone that you so irresponsibly answered? Did you provide her with groceries or additional meal plan account bucks? I'm just wondering how a young man with no contributions to anything in that room or the women in it would think it be acceptable to answer their phone."

Jeffrey's mouth hung open and rolled down to the floor and out the door as he passed me the phone.

"Hello, Daddy. Please don't fuss. He was just playing around."

"Nyla Howard, you are no man and I mean no man's play toy. Remember your worth baby. Please remember your worth."

"Yes, I will never forget it."

Oh, and then he was put on probation from his second job because he was helping me put together a bookshelf that I bought online and didn't realize that it took some serious assembling and time.

Jeffrey was always right there to help me with anything I needed, and let's not forget the countless "blue balls" he must have collected over the months of me being

203

just about ready to let him go all the way and deciding at the last minute to stop. That man had the patience of Job, but I still did not want to believe that he was ready for me or maybe I wasn't ready for him. Jeffrey scared me a lot. Friend, the thought of loving someone to the magnitude that I believed I could with him scared the hell out of me.

But now friend I do know what I was ready for; I was ready to continue to crucify Rashad's ass. No, I did not forget about him. My thoughts of Rashad were a different story from those of Jeffrey. I know relationships are tough. I know they can be a challenge, but Rashad rocked me to my core. I still couldn't believe he did me so bad. If only he could have stuck to our plans. If only he could have remembered all the things we had been through and conquered together. He wasn't the only one who had been there for me. I had been there for him on so many occasions. He forgot. He got comfortable and familiar. He decided to take me for granted, and we had a plan. We made a pact to stay pure for one another. Granted I had my purity ripped from me years before I met him, but at the age of fourteen when we met, I knew that he was the one for me. I knew it when he took up for me in the hallway of our middle school when a huge burly girl wanted to put my face through the locker because I was the new girl at the school. He was always there to protect me. I am still confused by the shit he pulled with all that cheating and lying and backstabbing. What an unloyal bastard.

You want to know why a good girl goes bad? Rashad River Jones and a few other negro variations of him. As I sat there pondering all I wanted to do to him, Keith Sweat sang to me, "I will never do anything to hurt you, I'll give all my love to you and if you need me baby I'll come running only to you." That damn flapping liar. He didn't do any of that. He took my heart and flattened it like a pancake.

That don't work, Friend. There is more *Nyla Revenge* coming his way.

Chapter 27: Finally, Our Time

As my day of Student Ambassador Training came to a close, I could only think of seeing Jeffrey. After our embrace that morning in the University Center, we agreed to meet up later in the week at Starbucks to talk about everything in more detail. Jeffrey was still in town for another week before he had to fly to California for his engineering co-op with a major engineering firm. I went home to freshen up because Sharon and I had agreed to have takeout in the student common lounge area of our dorm so that we could catch up with some of our dorm neighbors that we liked and possibly meet some new friends.

"Girl, Sharon, guess who I saw today?"

"Who? Jeffrey?" As she said his name, she did a roll-eye and smile combination.

"Umm, how did you know that?"

"Because he texted me and I confirmed for him where you would be this morning?"

"Oh no the hell you didn't, Sharon. Why would you do that?"

"Girl because you needed to talk to him and you, obviously, were not going to do it yourself, so I gave it a little nudge. SO did you all talk?" she inquired as she made a circle with two fingers and pushed her other finger through the hole.

"Sharon, you are so nasty. No, girl we didn't talk like that. We did talk though and are supposed to meet up later this week at Starbucks to talk about everything."

"Well, maybe you'll get to do the kind of talking I was talking about after that Starbucks meeting."

"Sharon, you are crazy, and why are you so concerned about me giving it up to Jeffrey?"

"Girl, Ny because that is what you have wanted to do since you first laid eyes on him at Orientation. You can try and fool yourself and him, but you're not fooling me. I see how much you love and long for that man. Even when you're around other men, and they could be the finest men on this side of the planet, you still have the longing for someone else. That man can only fill that void."

"Who, Carrington?" I said quickly to immediately interrupt her train of thought.

"No, tramp. Jeffery. You know that's what I was going to say and you know that is who you're longing for all the time. Be honest with yourself. Just tell the truth and shame the devil. God knows your heart."

"Ok, Sharon. Now here you go trying to bring God into this. Child trust me, God is not worried about me and my thoughts. He never has been."

"Wow, Nyla Howard. What are you talking about right now? You have beef with God or something?"

I just left that question unanswered and went back to a much lighter subject because the last thing I wanted to do is have another conversation about God. If God really even exists, he darn sure didn't care much about me. Hell, look at all the tragedy, loss, and abuse that has surrounded my life. No God, your Heavenly Father didn't give a care about me.

I smiled and chuckled, "Girl, Sharon don't get so deep tonight. Cause honestly I know I might long for Jeffrey as you said, but I can't stop fantasizing and thinking about my Poppa Idris- Mr. Carrington. That man is un-damn-forgettable."

I would fantasize a lot about my Christmas break. It was the most fun I have had in my entire life up to that point. I tried to block out his psychotic break because he was so good to me. When we arrived back to school a package came every day from Carrington for me. When we left Tampa to return to school, we stopped by his house and he had about five huge boxes for us to take with us. Only two could fit, so he said he would send the rest. When were far enough away, Sharon pulled over so we could look inside. It was everything from our last night together. All of the items in our own personal shoppers' room was packed in these boxes. All the shoes, clothes, makeup, undergarments. Oh my goodness this man was unreal. Sure he's a little crazy but who isn't. Hell, Dr. Newton would say I should give it all back and not speak to him again, but I say absolutely not. Dr. Newton would say, "Nyla, he's not good for you. This is a very volatile relationship that may cause you another mental break," but of course I don't listen. I'm in love with all Carrington has to give.

Then the huge flat screen caught our attention and brought me out of my fantasy.

News flash: Tallahassee native, Charles 'Chuck' Hadley, twenty-five years old was found dead in Tampa, Florida. Then it came… His picture flashed across the scene. He was last seen at Clearwater Beach area with two young women. Then the words… If you have any information about Charles Hadley or these young women he was last seen with, please contact Crime Stoppers at 1-800-NO-CRIME.

"Oh my God, Ny! That's Carrington's first driver! Two girls? They're looking for us- the police are looking for us," Sharon whispered to me as we sat there in disbelief. I held myself together long enough to get her under control.

"Sharon, stop it," I whispered back. "Please don't worry we are going to be fine. We didn't do anything wrong."

I walked away calmly and just made it to the communal restroom before I felt the rivers begin to stream down my legs. *Oh my gosh. Oh my goodness. Breath Ny, breathe please.* I couldn't control my breathing or my bladder. What was I going to do? What were we going to do? Did Carrington do this? Is that where he sent him off to that day? To his death. Oh my goodness.

Hi ho, hi ho. It's off to work we go! How many fish do you see? I see one, two, five and me. The itsy-bitsy spider went up…went up… where the hell did the damn spider go? Nyla, stop this; stop this. Remember what Dr. Newton said. You are strong. You are smart. You can handle this. You can handle this. Come back, Nyla, come back, a little voice whispered to me as I panted and breathed so hard that I could not feel my chest.

After what seemed like hours but was more like twenty minutes, I gathered myself, wiped myself off and went back to Sharon. Thank goodness for black. You couldn't tell what just occurred all down my clothes.

Friend, don't worry. I'm okay. Hell, at least I'm not bat shit crazy like Carrington.

I walked back to Sharon and looked at her with concern.

"Girl, are you okay now? Come on Sharon, let's get out of here."

We walked out cool, calm, and collected, but neither of us was really emotionally balanced at that moment. As we made our way back to our room, my phone rang. As I looked down, I almost felt like my heart was about to pop completely out of my chest. It was Carrington.

"Hello," I said trying not to sound weird.

"Hi, baby. I miss you."

I walked back into the living room area and closed the door behind me for some privacy and not to freak Sharon out. I never told her the entire story about my last night with Carrington and how he flipped out. I didn't think she could handle it, and I was right.

He and I talked for a little while until there was a knock at our door followed by, "Girls, its Nikki.

"Poppa. Our RA is at our door. Let me call you back later this week okay?" I said sounding like I couldn't wait to hear his voice again.

"Sure, Nyla. Have a great week. I look forward to talking to you soon."

Sharon came out of the room and we both looked a little alarmed. I opened the door for Nikki. She was our new Resident Assistant for the spring because our old one had to leave school at the end of the fall. There were scandals all around us. Our old RA was caught with drugs on campus. We had no idea she was on drugs bad like that,

211

and when our Dorm Director caught her, she was put out of the dorms and school. That was sad because she was super cool, but Nikki seemed okay, too.

"Hi, girls. I just wanted to give you our newsletter and let you know that if you all need anything, I am here for you."

"Ok, Nikki; thank you," Sharon said.

"I know that I introduced myself to you all at our dorm floor meeting earlier, but I wanted to meet everyone one-on-one to let you know that I am here if you need me."

"Thanks, Nikki. We definitely will," I said this time.

As she headed to the door, she left us with, "Well y'all have a good night and see y'all later."

We both chuckled as she shut the door.

"They think that we are all druggies now." Sharon said as I laughed louder now that she was completely gone.

"Child, yes," I replied.

After she left, Sharon and I decided to take showers to wash away all of our sorrows and worries. We sat there and talked for what seem like hours discussing all of our escapades. I was in the middle of making my infamous hot chocolate with marshmallows and caramel drizzle, when a knock came at our door. It had to be about one a.m. or close to it at that point, so we both stared at each other in fear and shock.

"Sharon," I whispered, "who in the hell could that be?"

"You think it's the police?" Sharon said with all the tremble in her voice.

"No, Sharon don't bring them up. Why would they be at our door at this hour? We didn't do anything wrong."

And then again a knock at our door with a voice that relieved us from our fears.

"Nyla are you in there? Please open the door. I really need to talk to you."

As Sharon and I stared at each other again, she smiled this huge and uncontrollable smile.

"Girl, open the door for your man."

I took a quick look in the mirror to make sure I could make him smile in my night lounge clothes. Betsy Johnson's two piece boy short set and Victoria Secret slippers.

Yes I do believe I was ready to open the door, I said to myself and corrected the huge smile on my face to one that didn't look so lustful and longing for him.

As soon as I opened the door, he dashed in hugging and kissing me with no shame at all.

"Umm Jeffrey."

"Nyla, Nyla! I love you; I am in love with you. The thought of being without you hurts me. It literally hurts my heart. I know that we said we should just be friends earlier. I know that I said I wasn't ready, but I am. I am! I want you. I want you!"

"Ummm, hello, Romeo. Can you please at least shut the door? The entire dorm floor is going to hear you," Sharon said as she stood there watching Jeffrey and sipping her hot chocolate as if this was a scene in her favorite romance movie that she could not take her eyes off of.

"Oh, I'm sorry. Sorry Sharon." He shuts the door and continues to beg for me to take him back or take him now or darn it, you know what I mean. He wanted me to want him, but I didn't know what to do. This back and forth with Jeffrey was beginning to make me tired. I loved the ground he walked on and he knew it since the first time I laid eyes on him. I tried everything to stop thinking about that man, to stop loving him, to stop falling for him harder and harder and deeper and deeper, but I couldn't and he knew it. He knew how I "fiend" for him. I don't know why he always had me like this.

"I love everything about you Nyla, and I want you. I want you. Every time I think of you being with someone else, I can't bear it. I know that I keep messing up with you, but have you ever loved someone so much that the thought of them makes you feel invincible? It makes you feel like you can fly- like nothing can penetrate you and you are unstoppable? That is how you make me feel. You make me feel like I can do anything."

"Jeffrey, just breathe, baby. I understand. I love you, too."

He hugged me again with the passion of five men in him. He kissed me and every part of my body felt it. Virginia shed a few tears of her own down there.

"Would you like some hot chocolate?" I asked him with such concern in my eyes.

As he said yes, I pulled him into me once more and kissed him sweetly and told him to make himself comfortable on the couch.

We had a full dorm suite, so that included a living area kitchenette and bedroom large enough to sleep four people, but we had it all to ourselves. Sharon and I were on our way into our bedroom to watch the Golden Girls reruns so we could laugh instead of crying about this Carrington ordeal.

When I was done making his hot chocolate, she smiled at us and said her good nights.

Jeffrey took two more sips of the hot chocolate, placed it on the coffee table and proceeded to kiss me. It was like he had been in the desert and was dying of thirst; I was his living well.

I stopped him gently and said, "Jeffrey, what is going on with you? What is up? In the fall, you were so unsure and you didn't know if you could be with me. Now, you are here and I am so confused."

"Nyla, do you not love me?"

"Yes, Jeffrey I love you. I love you with all my heart and soul and mind, but I don't want to keep being hurt by you."

"I'm sorry, Nyla. I'm so sorry. I know that I want you, but I keep telling myself that it is not going to work. That I am leaving in a few days for my co-op in California and you will be here and it would be too hard to do long distance and you might find someone else and I can't ask you to wait and oh my goodness please please marry me marry me fuck it let's just be together."

216

I chuckle because though I know he is serious, it is still funny to hear him talking about marriage and sounding so in love.

"Jeffrey Donovan, get it together. You sound like you're going through a midlife crisis right now. I want to be with you and surely marry you in the future, but umm- no sir, not now. Let's start with some TV and cuddle time. Okay? Calm down, baby. As much as I didn't want to admit it, I would wait for you forever and always. I love you Jeffrey."

And so we turned on the DVD player and watched one of my favorite movies, *Love & Basketball*. I fell asleep in his arms as he kissed my face.

When I opened my eyes, I thought it had to be a dream, but it wasn't and he was still here. Kissing my face. We kissed passionately over and over again and as he moved his kisses down the front of my body, I began to shiver down every part. It was real this time, and I was ready to go all the way with him and my wish was his every command.

He was so gentle and sweet and the songs that our body parts made were award winning. It was electrifying and the sleep and slumber that was once a part of my Saturday night was not anymore. Jeffrey led me every step of the way and Saturday Night Live was in full effect in Salley Hall Suite 2200.

"Nyla, are you sure you want to do this? He asked as he kissed my breast. We can wait. I promise I will wait for you, he whispered as he kissed my ear lobes. I love you so much, Nyla Howard," he proclaimed in between his lips locking with mine.

All I could continue to say, heck all I was able to say was, "Yes. Yes, Jeffrey I want this. I want you for as long as I can have you. I want this, please," I begged as if he had the last piece of carrot cake.

And just like that, and right after he protected us with his lifestyle penis raingear, Jeffrey was inside of me taking what I wanted him to have and giving me what I longed for since the day we met last summer during orientation small group.

He went slow and paid attention to my every move and groan. He knew what sound meant what and took pride in his work. This man was unstoppable and unforgettable. After what seemed like seconds, but had to have been twenty minutes, without notice, he pulled out and moved his mouth back down to my Virginia Brown again. Virginia was screaming in excitement. She had never ever been so alive. Nothing could prepare us for this. Jeffrey was a freakin' hero. I mean an absolute healer of my soul, and as he went back in me, still protecting us, it wasn't long before we both climbed to the peak of our mountain and our orgasms were two in one. He collapsed and so did I, but was I supposed to feel his juices flowing out of me?

"Oh my goodness, Jeffrey," I said still calm.

"Ny, oh my gosh. It broke; it broke. I'm so sorry."

With the horror in his eyes, I could only do one thing. I brought him close to me and rubbed his face and said, "It's going to be okay. It's going to be okay."

We laid on my couch in suite 2200 and drifted off to sleep. I couldn't think of a better night with a better person in a better place.

"I love you, Jeffrey Donovan."

"I love you, Nyla Howard."

Chapter 28- No New Friends?

Thank God this first week is over. Classes were so long and boring. I don't know if it was because it was the first week, but I was nervous that the semester would drag on the same way. Sharon reminded me at dinner that the first week is always boring because each class does the same thing: Attendance, Introductions, and Syllabus. It was so boring because you felt like you were hearing the same thing every day of your life for four to five days.

"Damn, have they ever thought about doing something different? Why doesn't the school make the professors switch it up some? I know they need to lay the ground rules, but can they be a little more creative please?" Sharon said and I laughed and shook my head in agreement.

It had been really busy that week, too because Sharon had decided to pursue being in a sorority full-time this semester. She knew that she had to have at least thirty credit hours at the school to pledge, but she was networking all this semester so she could be ready for the fall, in hopes that her desire to become a lady in Pink and Green would be a reality.

After that first week, Sharon met a pink lady in one of her classes and that was all she wrote. She was so involved in her soon to be sorority life that we hardly saw each other at night, but we stayed connected. I knew she would be gone most of the night, so we made a point to have our usual Honey Nut Cheerios breakfast with yogurt and banana together every morning. That was our date time. I couldn't complain though.

It all worked out beautifully for me. While she was out, I had my fun. My stable of boys, men, dudes and gentlemen was building to impressive proportions. I would be all over Tallahassee. My week would consist of studying and classes first, but then dinner in Killearn with Daniel, and cocktails with my bartender Boo at his family's bar off Capital Circle. BW3 saw a lot of me because it had so many men, especially during football season.

Jeffrey and I ended up talking again a few days after that night in my room and decided to just be friends. It didn't seem right for us to keep trying for something that wasn't coming together smoothly, so I did what any smart woman would do. I got busy with others. I had to before I let depression set in from not being with him.

"Hello. Is someone sitting here?" A deep voice sultry voice said and he immediately put me in the mind of Anthony Hamilton, one of my favorite singers. I slightly turned from my BW3 wings to acknowledge with a, "No."

I turned attentively back to my lemon pepper wings and curly fries and proceeded to pick up my next bit of succulent chicken.

"I'm Jasper."

"And I'm not interested, Jasper, in anything except these ten flat lemon pepper pieces of chicken."

"Oh, I apologize. Enjoy your chicken."

"Excuse me, Brad. Can I get my usual and another one of whatever Miss Lemon Pepper is drinking?"

My ears perked up because he knew my bartender, Brad. Now Brad wasn't my bartender Boo, but he was my homey from English 1102 class. Brad made the best drinks in Tallahassee. Yes, even better than Bartender Boo.

So how did he know Brad? I was curious but certainly played it cool.

As Brad looked at me for my order, I said," Yes, you can give me another Tanqueray and tonic just the way you made it the last time."

"Oh my, Miss Pepper what a bold drink. Long week?"

"No, I just like the way Brad makes drinks and ever since I started coming here he has made me different drinks and my T&T is the best thus far."

"Oh okay, well enjoy your meal. Maybe I can talk to you later when you're less consumed with Lemon Pepper."

"Maybe," I said as I slightly turned to meet my wings face to face and took another bite.

I could see he was still smiling.

BW3 had become my personal little hideaway spot that was in plain sight. Though it was so close to campus, certain people like Daniel didn't frequent there. He said it made him too weak, so he had to guard his spirit. I remember hearing him say that the first time and rolling my eyes. Thank goodness he did not see me. Why does this sexy handsome fine ass man have to spoil a great date with this spirit talk? One thing was clear, I wanted him. Mr. Texas bred Daniel could get me in my spirit and body.

It had been a few weeks since we first met at the back to school party, and Daniel had been a breath of fresh air that I needed so desperately. He was pure and sweet and full of humor and just what I needed at that time in my semester. The thoughts that rolled around in my head about him were all but pure; however, he was such a gentleman that he would not allow either of us to go too far. Heck, he wouldn't allow us to go a little far. I respected that about him, but it made me mad and horny often times, too. It was so damn sexy to have a man not want my body or at least pretend like they didn't want it.

Daniel was a true country boy and a real southern gentleman. He was raised right. He was an only child from a single mother who worked through blood, sweat, and tears to get him through life healthy in all ways. He was such a nice guy. He was true husband material. It was too bad that I was not looking for that in a man at that time at all. I had given up on them. Rashad made sure of that, so it wasn't worth me putting any more serious thought into it. Daniel was hella funny and such a cool person to hang out with. He cooked for me, took me out to dinner, movies, pool halls, golfing, and horseback riding. Whatever I thought of and wanted to do, he was down. He really loved spending the day with me, so we usually did at least three or four activities together, so when he texted me while I was in Philosophy class I was more than happy to respond.

"Hi, Nyla. What are you doing later this afternoon?"

"Studying and then hanging with you of course," I texted and smiled as I slapped on the charm.

"Great. See you at 8:00. I have something for you."

"Perfect and thank you in advance."

"Miss Howard. What is your favorite philosopher and why?" The sound of Professor Scott's voice shook me from my daydream. Philosophy is certainly a subject that I found interesting, but Professor Scott and his lectures were NOT. He made all the theorists and great philosophers sound like boring old lonely white men with no women or sex drives and I certainly needed just a little more stimulation to keep me interested. I certainly got it that day.

Professor Scott never asked questions or open the class up for discussion.

"Well, Professor Scott. One of my favorite philosophers has to be Socrates. He had a true passion for logic and was willing to die for what he believed in. There have been so many to study under him including another great philosopher Plato, and his Socratic method is still used in some version to this day. Though he was sentenced to death, he still died by his own choice. He demonstrates strength, passion and high intellect to me. That is why he is one of my favorite philosophers."

"Excellent explanation, Miss Howard. I look forward to reading your paper due this week."

As my eyes bugged out in surprise, I managed to say, "Thank you, and I hope you like it sir."

Oh my gosh. Paper what paper? Oh the reality of this Philosophy class kicked in and I realized that I better get somewhat serious about what I needed to do to earn this A.

Chapter 29—So long, Farewell!

As I walked out the lecture hall in the Williams building towards the FSU infamous fountain, I saw Daniel and he truly looked like a masculine beacon of light. He noticed me immediately and strutted over with such humble strides that made his presence bold but innocent. I promise if Daniel wasn't a virgin, he damn sure needed to be. He was this tall bright spirited young man with an electrifying smile that commanded your ears to listen to what he had to say. Daniel was a man after God's own heart, but certainly a man after my own thoughts as well.

As he walked towards me, I could do nothing but smile. He always made me smile. If only he knew the thoughts in my head, would he pour his blessing oil on me? I would welcome him and his oil. That seemed pretty erotic. This sacred sexy strong ass man and his healing oil. Please Daniel come and heal my soul.

"Hi, beautiful," he said so innocently.

"Good afternoon Daniel. Where are you headed?"

"I just finished one of my classes, now I'm headed to get something to eat and then a study group for my Research Methods class until I come to pick you up at 8. If you're not busy right now, you want to join me for lunch?"

"Sure. I would love to join you for lunch."

"Great. I hope I am not taking up too much of your time Nyla. I know you are very focused and I don't want to be a distraction."

"Please don't worry, Daniel. I am fine, and if I am off task it is my own fault, but let me ease your mind. I am fine and you are not a bad distraction at all."

He smiled. "So where would you like to eat?"

"How about Carabbas? I love that restaurant."

"Yes sure. I haven't been there yet, so let's go." He was just as excited as he always was when with me.

As my food arrived to the table, and the server walked off, Daniel hit me with yet another God inquisition.

"Nyla, do you believe in God?" Daniel asked.

I had been able to avoid the God conversations up to this point because our time together was always fun, but he always seem to slip it in and I was getting tired of it. *Damn, here we go with the Jesus stuff.*

"Umm, what type of question is that? Who doesn't?"

"And yet you still haven't answered my question."

Ugh. Daniel had a way of asking thought provoking questions. He always found a way to make our time together much deeper and meaningful than what I wanted it to be. Well, I didn't want to answer his question and I definitely didn't want to talk about God over dinner- especially when it's one of my favorite restaurants and meals. My delicious Carrabba's Johnny Rocco Salad would become wilted if we began this God and my beliefs about him conversation. Daniel knew exactly what to say to make me think deeper, and though I thoroughly enjoyed spending time with him, he was killing my buzz for him this time.

"Well, Daniel I'm sure God exists but he's not checking for me nor am I for him right now."

"Nyla, how did that feel coming out of your mouth because it sounded painful to me."

Oh my goodness this man. Would you stop? I thought as my face began to display my aggravation. He could tell and so he softened his tone.

"I like you, Nyla. I find you to be so intelligent and mysterious. I just want to know more about you."

"Well, Daniel. Talking about God is not going to get you more. It's going to get you cut off."

If he knew what was best, he'd just stop talking and let me enjoy Johnny. Well, he didn't know and he just kept talking. I felt like I was on some TBN special.

"Daniel. Listen. Everyone comes to God in different ways and right now mine might be on my back. In my short but meaningful time on this earth, I have seen people die before their time; bad people prosper at the expense of others and there is long suffering for those who constantly try to help. This is just a little of my family dynamics. What type of God lets one person endure all of this and then expect them to be thankful, grateful, or love him at all?"

He looked at me with such compassion in his eyes, but that just made me even madder, and so I continued.

"I really thought that I could care for you on a deeper level, but you are too damn pushy for me, and I don't believe this is going to work at all," I said with a smile on my face.

Once I was over something or someone, there was no reason to be upset and so I continued eating my delicious salad and listened to Daniel try and convince me not to cut him off. It was certainly too late for that and that was the last meal I would share with Daniel.

Dumbass I thought as I walked into my dorm room. Oh well. Another one bites the dust and it couldn't have come at a better time. It was right after Valentine's Day and before Mardi Gras. I had been blessed with so many great

Valentine's Day gifts and now I could go to New Orleans with my girls and not have to feel anything for anyone while I was there.

Since Jeffrey and I had decided to be friends, we had not been speaking, so I didn't have to feel guilty about him. Rashad's dumb self-centered ass didn't even know if I was alive or not and he still didn't have any idea that I knew about all his cheating. He just thought I was this sweet caring girlfriend giving him his space to shine. Like I said, dumb ass, and Carrington and I had a great agreement.

Because he loved me being in school, he didn't hound me at all. He would send for me all the time, but he wouldn't invade my space in Tallahassee. It was weird, but I liked it. I think he felt like himself around me because I didn't judge him after his breakdown over Christmas break. So hey, Mardi Gras here I come! Single and ready to mingle. I just need to get this Philosophy paper done and ace this Math test.

Chapter 30– Mardi Gras Baby

As we left the hotel, the doorman said to make sure that we all check out the bead shops before we get to Bourbon Street, so we did. I purchased a few cheap beads to have so my neck wouldn't be bare, but from what I heard from others who had been here before it was best to earn your beads.

"Well, Sharon. What do I have to do to earn beads?" I asked as we walked out of Aerobics together.

"Girl any and everything. Mostly men just want to see your breasts, but girl anything goes on Bourbon Street especially at night. You would be surprised what people will do for some beads."

"Ok then. I'm here for it. I'm ready for that type of fun. I need it."

The closer we got, I became more and more excited. I was ready for that type of fun.

As soon as we walked down Bourbon Street, the uniformed chanting took over. "Show your tits! Show your tits!" rang in the air, and there you had it- tits!

It was like nothing I had experienced before. At first, I was a little and I do mean a little nervous, but that was short lived. It was like a group of synchronized swimmers; all you saw was one blouse up, another one up then a V-neck up, and then another t-shirt up until the entire group of women standing in front of us were baring all for the crowds up high to see. It was a spectacle like no other. I had left Florida and gone to the land of the free. I loved this place. Hell, I could live here.

     Friend, I'm telling you, if you have not been to Mardi Gras, oh you had better go. You are sure to have the best time of your life, and you don't need to be ashamed about it.

     We walked from store to store and bar to bar. I bared all to the highest bidder. There was this couple with the most extravagant beads and all they wanted was to take a picture with me. That was innocent, but then they offered me five hundred dollars to take me back to their suite.

     "I'll pass. That's not my thing," I said still smiling at how sexy they both were.

     "How about a kiss?" she asked.

     "As fine as you are, no thanks."

     "What about her?" she said pointing at Kendra.

"Ken!" I yelled to get her attention before she put her mouth on another girl she had been talking to for a few minutes.

She immediately came over fussing. "Damn, Ny. I was just about to meet a new friend. What's up?"

"Ken. She wants to kiss you."

"Oh yeah." Kendra smiled.

"Yes, I do. You want these beads or more?" she asked Kendra with no shame.

"It's Mardi Gras, baby. I want whatever you're offering."

And just like that. Kendra was locked lips with this sexy ass stranger as her man watched in delight. He was so turned on by it that he couldn't even speak. It was a pretty sexy scene right there in the middle of the street as people just walked by looking and smiling.

After their lip locking exchange, she let Ken pick whatever beads she wanted and gave her the number and location to their hotel on a napkin with two hundred dollar bills wrapped inside. Kendra just nodded and kissed her again and slightly rubbed her man's penis, as she walked past him.

"Kendra! Oh my gosh!" Joy said as Sharon still had her mouth open.

"Girl you are fucking crazy," Joy continued to say. "I could never do something like that."

"Girl, never say never," Kendra replied as she showed us the two hundred dollars they gave her.

"So what's up? You going to their room later?" I asked.

"Nyla, hell no, girl. I have my limits now, but I couldn't help it. I had to taste her lips and after I saw the bulge in his pants, I had to at least touch his treasure. That damn man was packing, but I can't do that- especially with complete strangers. But they are a fine ass couple."

"Yes, they are!" we all said at the same time.

They looked like Pepa from Salt and Pepa and Treach from Naughty by Nature. Anybody would have wanted to be with them.

As we walked into another one of the Bourbon Street bars, I locked eyes with a guy that looked so familiar to me. He was light skinned and put you in the mind of Will Smith. I'm talking about the Will Smith from Independence Day, not Fresh Prince of Bel-Air. This dude was sexy and tall and had this biker military swag about him that made my eyes stay glued to him on and off for about twenty minutes. He commanded the room with his smooth walk that made him look like he was on his way to battle and knew he was going to win. He had a drink in one hand and was smoking something in the other. It wasn't a cigarette because those things turn me completely off, so as I continued to watch him, he watched back.

Of course, I wasn't going to approach him, and it seemed like every step he took towards me was being interrupted by some random chick trying to talk to him or some silly dude trying to talk to me. After a few no "thank yous" and "sure you can buy me a drink later," my Independence-Day-Will-Smith was almost to me. Gosh, he walked like he was floating on air just smooth out of this world. His glide was sho nuff confident, borderline arrogant, but I like that shit all the more.

Then it hit me as he smiled at me for what seemed like the fiftieth time. He looks like Elias. Elias Elliott from Tallahassee. You know Mr. & Mrs. Elliott who my mentor set me up to meet and they toured me all around Tallahassee. I know you remember them with the three boys and their stunning home in Killearn. Oh my gosh, if that is Elias, his pictures did him no justice at all. He was gorgeous and fine. His tall frame made keeping eye contact with him effortless, so when he was now in front of me I was elated, but you know I played it smooth. After all I'm Nyla.

"It took you long enough," I said playfully with all flirtation.

"I apologize. I got caught up a few times," he replied playing along.

"Oh okay. I almost left. I thought I wasn't going to get this moment." Oh, I was on a roll.

"I would have ran all over Bourbon Street after you." He smiled as if he knew that was the best reply ever.

It was good; I must admit.

"I'm Eli."

"I'm Nyla."

He looked as if he had just discovered the mystery we were both trying to solve for the past twenty plus minutes.

"Wait. Nyla? Where are you from? Or better yet what school do you attend?" he asked trying to get closer to solving the mystery.

"Umm. That's a lot of questions in a short period of time Eli. We just met. You could be a serial killer or something." I smiled.

He chuckled and said, "No, not at all. No it is nothing like that. I'm asking because I remember my

236

parents telling me about a young lady named Nyla who they showed around town for my godmother. She was her mentee or something like that."

"Are you Elias? Elias Elliott?" I exclaimed as we both felt accomplished for getting closer to the riddle being solved.

"Yes. Yes I am, but most people call me Eli."

"Oh my goodness, it is a small world. Your pictures do not do you justice, sir."

"Neither do yours, madam."

We both smiled in delight.

Damn, the chemistry was on point. It was like we clicked from locked eyes forty-five plus minutes ago.

"So Eli. I'm just sayin' we're at Mardi Gras. Show something!"

"What?"

"Um, sir. I did not stutter at all. Show something- tits or di.. what's it going to be?"

"Well, you know I don't have any tits, so… and right there in that crowded bar that fine as Eli unzipped and let me see what he was packing."

"Oh my. Yes you deserve five beads for that impressiveness. Way to go Eli."

"Thank you, but can I pick my own beads from
     around that sexy neck of yours."

With a nod, he went in. One bead and five kisses
     from neck to mouth to breasts.

Yes, it's Mardi Gras. Anything goes.

He went in and almost down.

"Oh my, Eli. You are something else. Come on
     back up here, sir."

"I thought anything goes, Nyla."

"Yes it certainly does, but I definitely need to have
you all night for that type of action." I said.

"I see, and yes I concur. Here's my hotel
information. I have my own room at the W off Chartres
Street. Come holla at me tonight. Ok?"

"Umm. I'll think about it," I replied playing hard to
     get.

"Ok, well here is a key. I'm going to put your name
on my room and I'll see you around 2. Cool?" he said
making the deal sweeter than before.

"Cool," I replied.

And like that he was gone, but we were far from
over. I had plans for him tonight. He was going to be the
one to make all my memories of the Florida scum drift
away. If his mouth worked on Virginia Downtown like they

238

did on my lips, I am going to be a happy woman tonight and forever more.

I knew he came from good roots and had a strong foundation. Mr. and Mrs. Elliott were great people and sweet to me. I could see myself being a part of their family in the long run. Might as well get it right the first time- marry for stability and not this emotional shit like love.

"Nyla. Come on girl; let's go. We aren't even half way through the bars." Sharon called.

"I'm coming!"

The rest of the night was a wrap. We drank and drank and drank and danced and danced and danced and drank some more. I can see why they needed Lent after this. They had to repent for all this sinning going on. Hell, they can repent for me cuz I don't feel bad at all. God not thinking about me, so hey! Bartender one more round of shots please!

And like that we were drinking again!

Chapter 31- Oh oh...

We had to be hung over for the next five days. Hell, at least it felt that way as I sat in my Biology lab and had to run out. I just made it there in time before I felt like my insides were being pulled out of me through my mouth.

"Oh my gosh!" I screamed out as if that was going to make this throwing up smell any better. It was crazy. I had been throwing up since that night with Eli. I tried to go to his room, but when I got there, he was passed out and I was too sick to even make it back to my hotel room. I threw up all over his bathroom, and had to call my girls to come and get me. Thank God our hotels were only a few blocks apart, so when they all got up a few hours after they got back to the room they were right there to meet me in the lobby of his hotel.

He was still passed out, so I checked to make sure he was still breathing and left. I thought for sure I would never hear from him again after the way I left his bathroom, but he was so nice about it the next day when he called me to see if I was okay.

"Uhh oh my gosh...what is wrong with me?" I spoke out again from the bathroom stall in the Biology building as I waited for this sickness to go away.

"Are you ok?" I heard from someone standing
outside of my bathroom stall.

"No, I'm not. I can't stop throwing up."

This really nice stranger went and got me a ginger
ale out of the vending machine and some crackers. "Here,"
she said as she slid them to me from under the stall door.

There was no decorum about my present position. I
was sprawled across the toilet like we were having our first
kiss on our wedding day.

I pulled myself up enough to grab the soda and
crackers. I took a sip of the ginger ale and a bite of the
crackers and had enough strength to open the door and
thank my saving stranger. She was one of my older
classmates who was so pretty and intelligent. She must
have seen me leave the classroom.

"Thank you so much." I said.

"You're welcome. I saw that you had been gone a
long time, so I just came to check on you."

"Oh my goodness. Thank you," I said begging.

"No problem. I know when I was pregnant with my
first child I sounded just like you did, so trust me I know
how you feel."

"Wait- pregnant. No, I'm not pregnant. I think my
friends and I had too much to drink last weekend."

241

She just stared at me. "Oh ok. I hope you feel better
soon."

But dammit, she had planted it in my head now. I
had gotten myself together and went back to lab. We only
had twenty more minutes left and as soon as we were
dismissed I went right to the drug store.

I couldn't even wait to get home. I took the test
right there in the Walgreens bathroom and what do you
know. Positive!

Chapter 32- Decisions, Decisions

It took me another week to get up the nerve to tell
Jeffrey. I told my girls, Sharon and Kendra at the same
time, but I swore them to secrecy and didn't want them to
share this with Joy. I loved Joy, but I didn't feel that close
to her to share this type of secret, especially since I wasn't
keeping it and she didn't believe in abortion.

As I dialed his number, I started to shake.

"Hello?"

"Hi Jeffrey."

"Hi, Nyla. How have you been? I've missed you."

"Jeffrey, I need you to come over."

"I wish I could, but I'm headed to work. Are you
ok?

"No, I'm not."

"What is wrong? Don't worry about it. I will be right over."

See that is the thing that was crazy about us. Jeffrey and I, since the day we met, have been connected in such a deep way that no matter what, we always knew when the other one needed them. He was my soul mate and I knew it, but we could not get our paths to cross and line up at the same time.

My thoughts were interrupted by his knocks on the door. I knew it had to be him, and as I opened the door I wasn't disappointed. Damn, he looked so good.

"What's wrong, Nyla?"

"Jeffrey, I am pregnant."

He stumbled back to the couch. He was speechless, and so was I. It was too quiet so I spoke.

"Don't worry; I made the appointment to take care of it, and Sharon is going to go with me. I just wanted to let you know."

"Why would you start a conversation like that Nyla? This is not like you're going to get a pedicure or massage. You're about to go have an abortion. Do you even care what I think? Why can't I go with you?"

"Well, honestly, no and no. I don't care what you think about this because this isn't your body and not to mention this isn't your decision about your life. This is a decision about mine. How can you act like you're ready for a child, Jeffrey? You don't even like to commit to picking a movie before we get to the theater. You don't even like to plan two days ahead let alone months or years ahead, which is what you have to do for a child. You haven't even been here since that night the condom broke. No, I *don't* care about what you think about *my* decision."

"Nyla, I love you, and I would love our baby. Please reconsider this?"

"I have considered this fifteen million different times and I am still coming up with no. No, I don't want to be your baby momma instead of your wife. No, I don't want to wait for you to get back from your co-op in the fall to help me with a baby instead of taking me with you so we can be together and experience this together. No, I don't want to give my mother the satisfaction of saying I told you so instead of making that witch eat every negative word she ever said about me. Jeffery, as much as I love you, I hate even stronger the idea of being a statistic. My mind is made up. I am not keeping it."

He just got up and walked out.

That wouldn't be the last conversation we had about this before my appointment date, but the night before the procedure was the worst.

"Jeffrey, I cannot be concerned about what you think. I understood that night of the big break, but you assured me that it was going to be okay. Now you don't want to understand me being pregnant and not keeping it. "

"Nyla, please just reconsider. I promise you we can make this work," He pleaded.

"What do you think I am, some sort of damn cliché? I will not be yesterday's news and as much as I loved you, I loved me enough to know that children are not and will not be in my near future."

"Why would you say that? Do you not think I would be a good father?"

"I am not saying that Jeffrey, but you have been a good, um- see I can't even say boyfriend because we jumped over steps. You and I were never a couple and couples should make these types of decisions together, but since I am single, I have made the best decision for me. I'm not keeping this."

I could hear him breathing hard and then words or mumbles filled with what sounded like tears streaming down the phone and then the dial tone.

He hung up on me.

Well, he made his choice, and we will probably not be the same because of it. How things change when you tell a man you're with his child? Hell, they act like you got yourself pregnant.

Oh well, he will be alright. I am the one that would have to deal with the burden of this decision for the rest of my life. I don't care if he is upset. Hell, I don't care if I lose him. I am not having a baby.

That would be the beginning of the end of us.

*

The next day came and went. Before I knew it, Monday was here and after being in bed the entire weekend recuperating, I was ready for the week. Staying busy was the best thing for me at that time.

Chapter 33- Fulfilling Fantasies

Only a week until Spring Break, and I cannot wait. This semester surely has shaped up to be a bit more challenging than my first. I came into FSU with quite a bit of dual enrollment and Advanced Placement credits, so I was expecting my semesters to be challenging. First semester wasn't bad academically and I was so thankful because with everything else falling apart around me, the last thing I needed was for school to go down the tubes as well.

However, this semester has definitely been more challenging. I am taking Statistics, Creative Writing, Introduction to Philosophy, United States History, Biology & Bio Lab, and Aerobics. I don't know what the heck I was thinking when I decided to take all these writing courses together, but it is too late to change them now.

What I don't understand for the life of me is why every single professor wants to give midterms and papers due on the same days. I mean, damn can they have a heart?

On another note, Sharon started the countdown on our Best Beach Bodies of 2001 calendar. I was getting more and more excited as the day to depart got closer.

The plan was for the three of us to road trip to Miami, stay at Kendra's house and then have her parents take us to the airport for our early Sunday morning flight out to Montego Bay, Jamaica. We would be staying at the Ritz Carlton, and we couldn't wait. We had less than two weeks before we left but a lot to do before we left Tallahassee.

*

I went to my spot, BW3 to clear my mind and take a study break, so I was certainly taking it light on the drinks.

Brad can I have another Malibu and pineapple please? It had been a few weeks since the procedure, and it was behind me with all the rest of the bullshit that came with it.

"So are you still determined not to talk to me lady?"

I knew that Anthony Hamilton voice from anywhere.

"Yes, actually I am. See, I have met you before a couple of times, and I just don't want to see you coming and make the same mistake again, so have a good night." I turned back to my drink.

"Damn, woman you are ice cold."

"Jasper, you just don't give up. My goodness," I said.

"See, I know I must have made an impression. You remember my name." He smiled with some hope in his voice.

"Let me just shut you down right now. I am not interested, Jasper. I am not interested in the least bit."

"Well, I am a very patient man and since we both like this spot, I can wait for your interest to grow."

"Ugh, you are so arrogant. Good night." I said growing disgusted with his arrogance.

"It certainly has been a good night. I got a chance to see the woman of my dreams again. Yes this has been a good night," he said as I turned my back to him.

I must admit that was smooth, but I was too into dissing him, so I couldn't show that I was touched by his game.

"Sir. You are too much. Really you are."

"Well, I am just being honest. Ever since I saw you for the first time and you dissed me, I cannot stop thinking about you, so I come here all the time looking for you. It has become a very expensive habit."

"Expensive. In what way?"

"You know we can't just sit at the bar, so I come and drink and eat and drink some more. All the while hoping you'll come through those doors. It gets to be expensive- especially since my boy Brad won't tell me when you usually come or if you've been here."

See that's why I like Brad so much. He never told my business and vice versa. I didn't know Jasper had been looking for me.

"Well. It's good to know you're a stalker too."

At that very moment, I could have sworn that I felt somebody staring at me and as I turned my head, I could see what I thought was the back of Jessie's (Jeffrey's ex-girlfriend's) head. What the hell is wrong with that chick? This isn't the first time I thought I saw her, but *if she's in here, she is going to get a great show tonight,* I thought as I turned back to Jasper who was looking more and sexier to me.

"So Mr. Stalker, what are we drinking tonight?" I asked in my typical flirtatious voice.

"Whatever you want," he said as if the world of alcohol was mine tonight.

"Brad." I waved to get his attention. Once he was in front of us, I asked him to make us his best shots. It was on from that point. My study break turned into a stop and the drinking and conversation began.

We talked, ate and drank until it was almost closing time.

250

"So, Lala." Jasper began.

"Yes," I replied.

"What's one of your biggest fantasies?" he asked.

I said, "Sex in the parking lot of a busy bar." That's what I wanted right then and there. Lala had taken over.

"Well, let's see if we can't check that off tonight," he said with a very confident smile on his face.

I motioned for the check from Brad. Jasper paid the bill immediately, we were headed outside, and just like that my parking lot bucket list item was complete. That man was definitely initiated into my stable of constant penis that night.

Chapter 34—SHARON'S SECRET

As I parked and walked to my dorm room, I was really hoping that Sharon would be there. I had to tell her about the asshole-turned-new-boo thang Jasper. At first, that fool made my skin crawl, but by the end of the night his sex game made up for all that crawling. He was so arrogant at first, and I didn't want to have to change my spot. After that parking lot action, BW3 has a new meaning for me. I just hope he didn't become a "bugaboo". I didn't want to be aggravated by him every time I went to BW3.

Unfortunately, she was not there. I knew that she wouldn't be because it was too early in the evening. She had been so dedicated to her pledging experience. She would come home long enough to perform the 3Ss: shit, shower and shave, but tonight was different and when she came in, she looked like hell rolled over.

Her tears awakened me as I jumped from my bed to run and hug her.

"Sharon, what's wrong?"

She had nothing to say, so I let her tears do the talking and I just listened as they washed onto my pajama top. I thought how our trip to Jamaica could not have come at a better time.

Chapter 35- Oh, Yes I Did

We made it to Miami in record time. Even though Sharon didn't share with me what was wrong with her a few nights before we left, we still had a blast. We kept our road trip rules and made it to Miami smoothly without any incidents. Once we got there, I told them to make one quick stop by Rashad's. It was time to end this charade once and for all.

"Rashad, I'm here. Open the door." You had to be buzzed in to get into his dorm. By the time I was on the second set of stairs headed to his floor (the 3rd floor), he was coming down the stairs.

Almost out of breath, he exclaimed, "Ny! Hey! What are you doing here?"

"Baby we have been so off lately that I had to see you. I wanted to see you before my trip." I lied to see what bullshit he was going to try on me.

"Oh baby." He grabbed me and pulled me close to kiss me. "Baby, I have missed you too."

But Friend before I could get lost in his eyes, lips, and embrace, "Her" words destroyed it all.

"What the fuck is this Rashad?" Her words punched me in the face as if it were Tyson setting his opponent up for a TKO.

That's all I remember before my version of Mike Tyson entered my body executed my best left jab and right hook to his face. And no it was not with my words but with my bare fists and all my power. Then I mortal combat swivel kicked his ass in his nuts leaving him temporarily paralyzed to set me free to head directly for her. I do believe I got one lick into her light bright ass before I was up in the air being carried away by two big ass boys at the

253

direction of Kendra. That's my friend and my ride or die homie, but I was so mad at her ass right then.

I heard Rashad saying "man get her the fuck outta here!" He said those words like he was running shit.

"Oh yeah! Oh yeah! Put me down and I'll show him who is getting the fuck outta here in a body bag or a stretcher punk ass! Man! Put me down" I screamed! I had some more fist to kicking ass combinations for both of them mutherfuckas.

Ken just kept saying, "I'm thinking about your future bitch" as these huge burley dudes carried me down the stairs and straight to our rental car.

I agreed with her in my head and began to settle down.

After that stop and all the drama, we went to Kendra's house, but before we left the next day, I had something in mind for Rashad. It would be of epic proportions because I couldn't get over Rashad and his cheating ass. Then he had the nerve to act like it didn't faze him that we were over. No problem. I knew what would phase him. I picked up my phone to put my plan in motion.

He picked up the phone on the first ring and actually sounded excited to hear from me.

"Hello, Nyla. Are you okay?"

"Hi, Willie. I guess you heard about what happened today, huh?"

"Yes, I did, and I'm sorry about all this shit. I told him he was a fool."

"Yeah right, Willie. You were probably happy about it."

"No, Nyla. I don't know why you would think that. You know I have cared about you since we were in elementary school. I know we haven't been the same since prom, but I never wanted him to fuck you over like this."

Bingo, I thought. This is it. *Now, execute the plan Nyla Howard.*

"Are you in your room?" I asked.

"Yes. I am," Willie said. I could almost hear him praying for my next response hoping that I was going to say what I did.

"Is it okay if I come over for a little while?"

"Yes," he said without any hesitation.

See, Willie and Rashad were on the football team together and live in the same dorm. I knew it would get back to Rashad by Willie's mouth or one of their teammates. It was about to be massive. That cheating fool would remember me for the rest of his life.

And so I went to Willie's room and gave him all that he had been dreaming of all these years- something Rashad never got the pleasure of having. I knew that would put a knife in Rashad's coffin. Can you imagine the woman you have loved for over five years won't have sex with you but did your best friend? Oh, it was one for the records, I must admit. Willie was good. I didn't expect that at all. He had stamina, picked me up and had me in the air. His doggy style technique was one to be awarded and was the perfect kickoff to my Spring Break trip.

CHAPTER 36- JAMAICA

Jamaica, Jamaica I will never be the same.

Hook me up, let me puff; kiss my wombs; spit that game.

Tell me I'm pretty, sexy, and fine as hell

Give me real good loving; make me scream, ring my bells.

Take away the sadness and feel it with licks

Give me all your island has to offer; yes, I want all your best picks.

Let me stay in ecstasy; let me know you are real.

When I leave here and until I come back, let me always feel your whip appeal.

I had a whole section of poems from Jamaica. As I sat on the plane, they just kept coming to me. Oh my goodness, friend, because of Spring break in Jamaica, I will never be the same. I know you have heard me say that before, but I am serious! Jamaica is where I belong. I think I am going to move there next year. To hell with America and all the men here; I am sure I can find a good school to go to. Maybe I can do online school and still graduate from my beloved FSU. In any case, I want to see Jamaica every day for the rest of my life. From the time we got off the plane to the time we got back on it, there were "No worries Mon." The Jamaican people lived by this creed, and I felt no worries the whole time I was there.

As I sat in my window seat, first class next to Kendra with Sharon across the aisle from us and Joy sitting next to her, I just smiled and laid back to ponder on the beauty of Jamaica. Then as soon as our plane landed state side and I turned my phone off of airplane mode, the text messages and voice messages flooded in.

First text: *Hi Nyla. It's Jeffrey. I can't stop thinking about you, and I know we said we should just be friends. I need more. Please call me as soon as you can. I really need to see you.* What the flip? Why would he send this to me knowing where he left me less than a month ago? Now this bastard wants to talk. Oh now he has had a damn revelation. For what purpose and why would I call him and talk to him. Hell, no. Jeffrey Donovan can go suck it. I don't want to talk to him.

Then there was another long stream of messages from Carrington. *Hello gorgeous. I know that you are still away, but I wanted you to know I missed you, and I hope you and your girls enjoyed my gifts to you in Jamaica.* Hell, yeah we enjoyed it. Carrington hooked us up. At check in, Tony, the front desk agent, didn't ask us for a method of payment. We prepaid for our room, but we all thought that we should still have to put a credit card down for incidentals. But hey, we didn't complain and just went about our vacation. After all the water sports and excursions, we just knew our final bill would be over a thousand or so. Since we didn't receive a final bill under the door, we went to the front desk to check out, and that is when they informed us that all of our charges had been taken care of by Mr. Carrington Brown. All we could do is smile.

"Well thank you all for an amazing stay. We really had a wonderful time." We all expressed our gratitude to Barley at the front desk, and walked away smiling big.

Kendra said, "If you haven't given that man any yet, you need to make it happen soon."

Joy was like, "Who does that? I don't know any man who would do that for me, let alone my friends." I knew he was crazy, but I could handle his kind of crazy.

The next text message came from crazy girl. *Nyla. This is Jessie. Umm I just want to know why you are still messing with my man. Stay the fuck away from him.* What the hell is wrong with that girl? She is completely obsessed, and I don't know what the hell she is talking about. She's crazy. This isn't the first message she's sent me like this. I have reported her, but campus police say they can't do anything about her. She calls me all the time from unknown numbers and just hangs up or drives by my dorm or classes so I can see her then just speeds off. She's touched in the head, but I wasn't going to let her spoil my good mood. I moved on.

I listened to my voicemails next, and the first voice mail made me laugh out loud. *You are a slimy bitch, Nyla Howard. How could you? How could you?* Then, the next message and the next one and by the tenth message, I couldn't control myself. That fool almost made me tinkle on myself because I was laughing so hard. I don't know

259

why he would even mess with me. He knew I was crazy. *How the fuck could you do that to me Nyla? My best friend. My best friend. You have no fucking soul. I can't believe you would fuck my best friend.*

"Ha!" I said to the phone. "You better believe it piece of shit." I wish he would call me again. He better be glad I was away from this phone, but mission accomplished.

Then the next message came through. *Hi, Nyla. It's your mother. Call me.*

I will not, I thought as I immediately deleted that message and kept going to the next one. *What the fuck Nyla? Did you take my money out of my bank account too?* Oh wow; I was still laughing to myself. I forgot about that one. On our way down to Miami, I sure as hell did. I wanted some spending money, so I took five hundred from him. Yeah that seemed about right, but then he had the nerve to act like he didn't care when I saw him that day before we left. So on our way to the airport, I took five hundred more. Fuck him! He deserved it and more. Serves him right. I bet he'll think about the next time he wants to cheat on someone. *Fuck him,* I thought as I let out another laugh. Ken, Sharon, and Joy just kept staring at me, so I let them hear the messages. My girls got a good laugh out of all his messages, too. We laughed all the way to the car as we headed out the airport.

Chapter 37- VEGAS Dreams

We dropped Kendra off and headed back to Tallahassee. We got back there in record-breaking time to get a quick bite to eat and get ready for Monday. After a full day of classes, I sat in the dorm common area, staring at my calendar. I kept telling anyone that would listen my perspective about professors.

"I'm serious! Professors are here to make our lives HARD. Just difficult for no reason at all." I complained. Everybody just chuckled and said, "Girl, Nyla stop! You know you are going to be fine." I was serious, but no one took me seriously. Everybody knew my grades, so I didn't get any sympathy from my dorm family. They made me laugh though, so I went back up to my room in a much better mood. I had to get a schedule together to get through the week because within a week of being back from Jamaica, I had three exams. The most challenging of them was definitely Biology. As I heard the phone ringing, I tried to ignore it the first time. On the second round of rings, I couldn't help it and had to answer.

"Hello?" I sang with a little annoyance in my voice on the phone.

"Hello, my beauty. How are you this evening?"

"Carrington, oh my goodness. To what do I owe this call? I thought from your message that you were out of the country for a few more weeks visiting family."

"Yes, I was supposed to be, but I had to come back early because I have to be in Las Vegas for the next five days; so what do you say?"

"What do I say about what, Poppa?"

"What do you say about coming to Las Vegas with me?"

"Carrington! I wish I could, but I can't miss that many days of class."

"How about you come on Thursday after your last class?"

"That would give us a nice amount of time together and I can extend my trip until Sunday to be with you?"

"Oh my gosh, Carrington. Of course I'll come babe. You know I can't resist an opportunity to see you. It's been almost a month since I saw your face. I miss you, Babe."

"Nyla, you know I miss you. How is everything going with school?"

"Great, of course. Thank you for asking. Speaking of which, though. I have to go and finish studying for my Biology test tomorrow. Can I call you back later?"

"You can call me whenever you want to Nyla. You know I'm here whenever you want or need to talk to me. You're my sweetness. I miss you beautiful."

"Aww, Carrington I miss you, too. I'll call you back before I go to bed."

"Okay, gorgeous. No pressure. Call me when you can. I'm into you, Queen."

"I know it, Baby. I'm into you, too. Talk to you later."

As I hung up the phone, I started to daydream about Vegas. Oh, this is going to be the shit! Yes, that man knows how to spoil a woman. Wait- what the hell am I thinking? Carrington might be a damn murderer. What if he gets me to Vegas and I never make it back?

Forget that. I'm going. Heck, at least I'll die happy.

Let me stop that because Carrington has never done anything to hurt me. Maybe himself or someone else, but not me. He has always been such a sweet and generous

263

man. He sends me care packages full of goodies at least once every two weeks.

See, the sources of Carrington's endless streams of money was unclear. I know that he owned a few companies like the Aldo Shoe store where we met and a couple of fast food restaurants and plenty of houses. Carrington had family in the Bahamas and the UK, so he stayed traveling to both places often during the year.

I respected all of his hustle spirit because he kept his streams of income flowing which meant more for me to play around this world with, and I loved it.

Carrington was extremely generous. He knew I just lost my father last year, so he was more than willing to provide me with anything that I needed, though that really wasn't much. That just meant that I could spend my money on any and everything I wanted to spend it on. Sometimes, I felt like it was a payoff for not going to the cops about Chuck, his dead driver, but hell he didn't know that I even knew about him being missing. Carrington was a lot of fun with endless pockets, so I was not going to mess that up with unnecessary questions and accusations. Hell, he wasn't the first killer that I knew and probably wasn't going to be the last.

Focus, Ny, focus. I told myself as I thought about my Idris and our trip to Vegas. Heck yes; this would be my reward for acing my Biology test tomorrow, so now all I have to do is ace it.

It would only be two days before I headed to the airport for Vegas, so I had to make sure all plans were in order.

CHAPTER 38—Sibling Love and Wonder

"Hi, Ty. What's going on?" My twin must want *something* since he's calling.

"Ny! Where the hell have you been? I thought I was going to have to hitchhike with some trucker named Bubba to Tallahassee to find you.

"Ty, really. Why so dramatic? I just talked to you last weekend."

"Well, I was calling you to tell you about what we found in Gran's house."

"What did you find? Damn, Ty get it out."

"We found Liv's journal. Well, I found Liv's journal."

"What are you serious? How did you find Olivia's
   journal Tyler Howard?"

"My goodness Ny. Why the formalities? Damn my
   entire name?"

"Yes. Spit it out Ty."

"Well. Gran sent me up to her attic to find some old
picture album that she had been looking for and while
looking through some boxes, I found it wrapped up and
sealed tight."

"Did you open it?

"Umm, well."

"Ty! Did you open it?

"No, Sissie. I didn't open it. I was too nervous
about what I might find. I was honestly too scared to read
it."

"I'm sorry for screaming at you and I understand.
   Did you tell anyone you found it?"

"No. I didn't tell a soul. I wanted to tell you first
   and see what you wanted to do."

"Umm. Just hold onto it and bring it when you
come next month for the event. I really don't want either of
us to read it alone."

"I know Sissie. It is going to be emotional. Do you
   think she tells us why she did it?"

"I don't know, Ty. I sure hope so." And there came the tears from both sides of the phone. We just cried and cried and cried some more.

"I still don't understand, Sissie. Why did she have to do that? Why couldn't she let anybody help her?"

"I don't know Ty. Suicide doesn't leave us with a lot of answers- just a bunch of questions."

> "Promise me you won't open it until we are together."

> "I promise, Ny. I won't open it until we are together next month."

"Ok. I love you, and I'll talk to you later."

"I love you too, Sissie."

I sat there and just wept some more. My sister, Olivia was everybody's favorite. She was the apple of everyone's eye. When the police found her body in that car, we didn't believe it. Nobody believed it. She was so pretty, inside and out. She had so much going for herself. She was at the top of her class, in so many clubs, and one of the best cheerleaders on the squad in school. She was the life of the party, and she really did a great job of keeping it together after Baby Dyll died. She even had a decent relationship with our mother. She was the epitome of a saint. When she started acting strange her senior year of high school,

267

everyone became overly concerned. She hated the attention and just wanted us to stop being so overprotective of her, but nobody could stop that. She was Olivia the princess. Her death was ruled a suicide by accidental overdose. I never believed that and always needed more answers. Liv was such a happy person. She was so positive and always saw the best in herself and everyone around her. When she died, my mother and my relationship really became challenging. Honestly, I hated the woman. I blamed her for it all. Olivia was my big sister, best friend, advisor, tutor, hair stylist and role model. I loved every part of my sister.

The phone interrupted my thoughts, and this time I was thankful. I felt myself drifting away into a place I couldn't afford to go to, so I answered on the first ring to hear Sharon asking me to catch a bite to eat with her. Since she was always gone and I was headed to Vegas the next day, I jumped at the opportunity to eat with my girl.

"I'll meet you in twenty," I said as I hung up the phone, grabbed my clutch and headed out the door.

Chapter 39- Hot & Wet Vegas

The plane ride back from Vegas was smooth and relaxing. The perfect opportunity for me to relive all the fun I had in my head. You know Sharon couldn't go because she was completely into her Pink and Green thing, so I didn't bother her. She was going to be so mad that she missed this trip. When I tell you that Carrington set it out Big Willie style for me, I mean it. Let me tell you he did.

He met me in the airport and had a car waiting for us to go to the Bellagio Hotel. This was my first time in Vegas, so I was too anxious and excited to get out and about on the Strip. I had done some research before I got there, so I knew most of the places I wanted to go to, and Carrington was more than willing to take me. We rode with the windows up because it was certainly the middle of the day and neither one of us was used to this type of heat, but I heard that it did cool down at night. I didn't care about the temperature. That just meant I didn't have to wear a lot of clothes and we were both fine with that idea.

The first thing we did was check into the hotel.

Friend, when I tell you my mouth dropped under the ground when we pulled up to the Bellagio. This hotel was larger than any hotel I had seen before, and the lighting and fountains surrounding it were exquisite. As we pulled up,

Charles, the valet, opened my door and welcomed us. He then turned us over to Jarvis, the Doorman, who escorted us to our personal Bellman, Joseph, who walked us right to the front of the exclusive member line where Rebecca was waiting to greet us. Joseph stepped back with our bags and let us know that everything would be waiting for us in our suite once we got there.

    "Welcome, Mr. Brown. We have certainly been
        expecting you, sir."
What the heck! I thought. This man is known
        wherever he goes.
    "This must be Miss Howard. Welcome, Madam.
We will take great care of you while you are here with us."

    "Thank you," I said pleasantly, trying not to look so surprised by the fact that Rebecca, Front Desk Expert, knew who I was by name. I knew Carrington had something to do with that. He is such a charmer and was smitten by me. I am sure that he made sure everyone knew who I was well before today.

    "Mr. Brown. We have upgraded you from our Bellagio Suite to a Penthouse Fountain View Suite since you are here celebrating with your love."

Oh Rebecca is really pouring it on strong, but what is this special occasion that she obviously knows about that I don't. Love? Huh? What the heck is Becky talking about? But what the heck. I roll with it, and just smiled.

"He certainly is an amazing man, Rebecca." I smiled and stared at him as he continued to conduct our check-in business.

"Mr. Brown. Is there anything I can get you right now before Joseph shows you to your room?"

"No Rebecca. You have been outstanding. Thank you."

"It has been my pleasure to serve you Mr. Brown & Miss Howard. I believe that you all will enjoy your time here with us, and please let me know if there is anything that we can do for you all to make your stay here with us at the Bellagio more perfect."

As we proceeded towards Joseph who was waiting attentively for us, Carrington slipped him a bill and said, "Joseph, I will take it from here. Just have those items ready for me when we arrive to the room. I would like to show Miss Howard around your beautiful hotel myself."

"Yes sir," Joseph said. "Here is my card sir. Please let me know if you all need anything at all."

They exchanged nods; Joseph was off and so were we.

Friend, when I tell you this hotel was gorgeous! The exterior was nothing compared to the inside.

After we left the front desk area, there are several paths you can take through this hotel. Of course, one led to the Casino. Another to the pool area and yet another to the restaurants and other attractions. The Bellagio had well over five restaurants and a pool that was absolutely breathtaking. There were fountains in different areas of the hotel and perfect artwork and sculptures for picture taking. Carrington and I took the best selfies and enjoyed being close to one another at all times.

We heard about the daily fountain show outside the hotel and looked forward to catching it while we were there. Fran, the concierge, told us that the show is about fifteen minutes and starts at eight o'clock nightly. She said that there is over seventeen thousand gallons of water in the air from the fountain at any given time. It was a true wonder to see, and I was looking forward to it. She was happy to tell us about the award winning buffets in the Bellagio and expressed that we must wake up for the breakfast one, which would have everything from your regular sausage, bacon, pancakes and oatmeal to crab legs, eggs benedict, corn beef shredding carving station alongside a steak carving station as well. The food display and selection was beyond impressive. I had never been a buffet person, but the description of these buffets made me salivate at the descriptions alone.

Once pointed in the direction of the restrooms, I told Carrington I would be right back. It took me almost thirty minutes in the bathroom because it was so beautiful. I mean luxurious. Who would have known that a public restroom would be so perfect? With the intricate details on the stall doors, to the marble like floors and chandeliers, I felt like royalty. I just walked up and down the restroom main floor. I just couldn't believe how sophisticated this hotel was and from what I was told, they were all like this. I felt like I was in another world. After the tour of the hotel, Carrington and I walked the strip. I felt like I had my own personal Vegas tour guide. Carrington knew about all of the hotels, their history and their highlights. One of my favorites was definitely the Bellagio and Stratosphere for the Stratosphere Tower rides. Caesar's Palace was definitely a sight to behold with all the gold columns and fixtures. Vegas just gave complete way to all fantasies and imaginations.

The first night there we went to dinner in the hotel, saw one of the Cirque de Soleil shows, and then took a helicopter ride tour of the strip. It was a magnificent night. The helicopter ride allowed us to see all the bright flashing lights. All the illuminated signs just made the ride feel magical. Carrington told me all about his times in Vegas. He was really lucky and always hit it big.

"Nyla, since this is your first time in Vegas, whatever I make tonight is yours." He said it so casually.

"Umm, Carrington. Can we put this in writing?" I chuckled but was serious.

"I am serious, and my word is everything. Whatever we make from this hundred dollar bill is yours to keep."

As we walked back towards our suite, he never stopped touching me.

From him holding my hand to his arm around my waist or shoulders, he never stopped his physical contact. As soon as he opened the doors to this beautiful penthouse suite, I attacked him. I figured I better get some before he had another episode like in Tampa.

"Damn, baby. That was a new shirt." He chuckled.

"You can afford another," I said as I continued to rip his shirt off and then his linen white pants.

He slowly stepped away from me with lust and surprise in his eyes.

"Nyla. Are you ready for this?"

"Carrington, the real question is are you?" And it was on from there.

For the next three hours, we explored every part of our bodies in every area of that suite. On the bed, on the floor, in the Jacuzzi tub, on the table, all over the glorious Bellagio Penthouse suite. He made me scream his name and carve my initials in his back in ecstasy. I knew we would be a perfect sexual match, but I didn't know it would be this damn good. Carrington made me feel like a gymnast and I came all over his body.

*

We managed to make it out of the room a few times that weekend, but we made use of his lodging dollars. That room was christened N.C. style, so when it was time to leave I was not too happy. Getting off the plane in Tallahassee that night was hard. I just wanted to forget about Tallahassee and all that it didn't have to offer me, and then I decided- Fuck 'Em. Like Martin in *You So Crazy*. Fuc 'em girl, fuck 'em. Jeffrey Donovan would get no more of my damn thoughts, so as I exited the airport doors, I spotted Sharon and flaunted a new perspective.

"Girl you got some penis. I can see it all over your face. She screamed as we got in her car.

"Girl, did I!" was all that I could say.

Chapter 40- Physically & Emotionally...SICK

Friend, I don't know what the hell I picked up in Vegas, but I felt like crap. I had a runny nose, sore throat, achy body, watery eyes, and mucus coming out of me that was a brownish green with hints of yellow. Just disgusting. I tried all my home remedies and none of them worked. I spent the first weekend in bed drinking hot-totties with top shelf whiskey and rum; I knew I would be right as rain. I even called home to make sure I had the remedy just right. After listening to Ty and Josh try to tell me how to get it just right, my uncle Norman took the phone and the real lesson began.

"Okay, Ny, this what you do. First you need honey, lemon, your choice of brown or white pure full proof liquor, and peppermint. You need to squeeze the lemons into a pot, add the honey and peppermint with about a half cup of the alcohol. You want to have it on a low temperature because you don't want it to get too hot. Once it is nice and hot, take it off the stove and pour it into a nice mug. Sip it slow and make sure you drink all of it. Does this all make sense?"

"Yes, Uncle Norman. It does."

"Okay, so do that, put some Vicks vapor rub on your chest and under your nose and put on a sweatshirt. Take one aspirin and go to sleep. You'll feel much better in a few days."

I felt better the next day, but it wasn't enough and after a day or two, I felt like shit spit on again. Finally, after about two weeks, I decided to go to the doctor on campus. I had bronchitis and a God awful cold. So after three hours in the campus ER, an IV of fluids, and about five prescriptions of meds to take, Sharon and I headed back to our dorm room.

As we walked in, I saw the light flashing on my dorm phone, which usually signaled to us that there was a message waiting. Though I was still a bit sore and achy from all the poking and probing at the clinic, I made my way to the phone to retrieve the message. My heart sunk at the sound of his voice. It had been over two months since we talked, and we did not end on the best terms.

Hi, Nyla. It's Jeffrey. I am breaking inside and need to talk to you badly. I am sure you don't want to hear from

me, but I really need to hear from you. I miss you and pray
that you will please call me back. I love you deeply.

I don't know why and I don't know how, but the
tears sprung up and out like a raging body of water that just
broke the dam that was holding it captive.

"What in the hell? Who in the hell was that? What
is wrong, Ny?" Sharon asked, looking more and more
alarmed.

"I can't talk about this right now, Sharon. I just
want to go and lay down. I know it's too early to take
another pain pill, but please wake me and give me one as
soon as it is time. I am going to go lay down."

"Okay, Ny. No problem. I'll be in here if you need
me."

I threw my hand up at her as I continued to walk
into our bedroom. I grabbed my journal and began to write.

Dear Jo... Jo is the name I gave my journal. I didn't
like Dear Diary or Dear Journal, so I called her Jo.

Dear Jo,

It has been a long time since I wrote in you, but I
just had to get you caught up on my life and everything
occurring in it. Rashad and I are officially over. I found out
that he was cheating on me and this chick wasn't the first
one. After looking in his wallet, emails, and room, I

discovered that the bastard had a Hoe Stable of his own. I wish I could say that I don't feel bad for what I did to him, but that would be a lie. I do feel bad for a couple things that I did to him, but not enough to regret any of it. He deserved it, Jo.

Did you know that he got someone pregnant and had a baby on the way? Yes, when I found that out, I lost it, so I hope you understand that everything I did to him was warranted. I'm stuck in bed for a few days with the flu, so I'll talk to you later about Jeffrey Donovan. It is still fresh and still hurts deeply. I'm sleepy.

Love you Jo,

Nyla

The next day was spent in bed. I got a lot of writing done.

Hey Jo,

Walking into that office of the clinic made me relieved and angry all at the same time. I thought he loved me no matter what. Hell that is what he said. Well of course until I told him I wasn't having his love child. Why in the world would I want to be that girl? I refused to be the girl who went away to college and came back home because some dude knocked her up. He would be free to continue to live his life while I would be stuck with a "snotty nose." No thank you at all. Maybe I will want some snotty nosed kids in the future, but that was certainly the far and distant future. I wanted to be free for as long as I could be free and a kid at this age was going to make me a slave. I tried to explain all of this to him, but he didn't want to hear any of it, so why in the hell would he be calling me now. He broke my heart.

Ny

After a couple of days of being in the bed, I jumped up and got my shit together. I could not let this flu or the constant thoughts of Jeffrey keep me down. Sharon had been there for me all weekend. She made sure I took the meds and ate some food. Didn't want to do much and I couldn't stop thinking about Jeffrey, and he was right. It had been about two months since we last spoke and it wasn't for me trying. I called him and left several messages, but it was obvious he didn't want to talk to me because of my decision to abort. As far as I was concerned, he could kiss my ass now with no hope of reconciliation. I had certainly cried my last tear for Jeffrey Donovan this weekend. So my declaration on this day is a Fuck Him Declaration.

I declare today, April 4th 2001, and forever more that Jeffrey Donovan is a punk azz whore.

He can call all he wants and beg all he pleases, but he
will never ever kiss above my knees.

I thought he was the one and knew he was it until he
left me alone to feel like shit.

SO this is my declaration, and I say it loud and proud,

Jeffrey Donovan can kiss between my darkest clouds.

Chapter 41- I See Pink & Green

The next week was spent preparing for Sharon's
coming out. She had been working tirelessly to be one of
those Pink and Green people, and her day was finally
coming. She wasn't staying in our dorm this week, so I had
a "Sharon-coming-out-sweat-shop" set up. I had glue guns
going, needle and thread for personalized initials,
scrapbooks and lots of letters and paint. I contracted out
some of our dorm friends to help, and that is when they told
me that Joy was on-line with her, too. They knew that they
had to tell me because I would have been so mad at Joy for
not helping with all of Sharon's gifts. When I found out, I
went and got some gifts for Joy too.

Kendra and Ty came up that Thursday and were able to
help me put together their pink and green baskets. We
hooked them up. The baskets had everything to begin a
pink and green life. They had pink and green everything:

pens, pencils, stationary, socks, shoe strings, t-shirts, jackets, paddles, stuffed animals, bags, hats, sunglasses, pictures, mugs, glasses. You name it, we got it for them.

It was so much fun getting everything together for them.   Ty brought Olivia's diary but we both decided to wait to open it. We didn't want to be so emotionally destroyed that we couldn't be there for Sharon and Joy on their big day, and before you knew it, the clock said three a.m. We attempted to get some sleep because the next day was going to be exciting.

Chapter 42- APRIL COMING OUT...

The day was finally here, and Sharon was so nervous. She came home early to have Ty do her makeup and Kendra did her hair. We sent her off in style! Kendra, Ty, and I got to the Union early; this was no ordinary union day. This was the day that my bestie was coming out as a pink and green lady. I was so happy for her and Joy. Not only were we all friends, the two of them were line sisters. The whole day was a hit and Sharon was a natural. She stepped like her life depended on it. She started so many of the steps and we were screaming to the top of our lungs for her. We were so pumped for her and Joy. Joy wasn't much of a stepper, but she could sing her ass off. She sang all of their songs and had the entire crowd screaming her name. There were eleven girls that crossed. Sharon was the tail, #11, and Joy was her front- #10. The show was pretty good- especially considering I always heard that this group of women were known for being too prim and proper to step hard. Well they proved some people wrong that day. Everybody knew the after party was going to be a blast. It was bound to be a hit with all the excitement that day in the union.

Chapter 43- Blind RAGE

The after party after the after party was the four of us at our Waffle House. Tyler had a friend in Tallahassee that he went to see after the step show in the union, so we wouldn't see him again until the next day or two. We were laughing and talking about all the people who came out and was just amazed at the love the community showed for the pink people.

When Jeffrey walked in, I almost fell over. I could not believe that it had been so long since I actually saw him. It had to have been a couple of months- you know, since I had the procedure and we had the big blow up. I didn't care though. Well at least I acted like I didn't care.

He just looked at the four of us as if he was in a state of shock.

"Nyla. Excuse me. Can I talk to you for a minute?"

"Excuse me," Joy exclaimed.

I look puzzled at her, but didn't think anything about it, and just said, "It's okay, Joy. I'm good. Yes Jeffrey?" I got up from the table and followed him out of the Waffle House and away from the building near his car that wasn't in direct eye contact with my girls.

"What? What Jeffrey?" I asked impatiently.

"Nyla. I know we haven't spoken in a while, but I have really missed you. I didn't realize how much until I walked in and saw you sitting there. How have you been?"

"Jeffrey. Hell no. Not tonight and not right now. You are not going to do this here and now. I am fine. Thank you for asking as if you give a shit." I could feel myself getting upset.

"Nyla, we just ended on such hard terms," he began.

"Jeffrey. I am fine and I don't want to talk about this, so take care."

"Wait, Nyla. Please, please don't leave. Please don't go. Please not yet. I have tried everything that I could to get through this. I tried respecting your wishes for me to stay away from you, but please just listen."

284

"Jeffrey, you have two minutes and I mean two."

"Okay, Nyla. I love you and I can't stop. I have tried. I have tried. I started dating again and that didn't work. Then I met someone and she seemed nice enough. I am sorry that I didn't know that you all knew each other."

My eyes went from aggravated to concerned and then pissed.

"Umm, Jeffrey, your two minutes are moving faster than ever. You better start explaining please. What do you mean *knew each other*?"

"Nyla, I have been dating Joy for the past month. I didn't know that you all were friends. I didn't know."

I stumbled a little bit, and he rushed to try and help me. I had the car. I didn't need his ass.

"Don't fucking touch me Jeffrey: don't touch me! What the hell do you mean you've been dating Joy? We've been friends all year. How could you not know that we knew each other? How could you not know that we were friends?" I almost started screaming.

"I swear to you I didn't know. I have never seen you all together and didn't know her name was Joy until you said it in the Waffle House just now. She told me her name was Destiny."

"Yeah her middle name is Destiny. That bitch." I screamed.

Now I was pissed. Forget that- I was beyond pissed. I was livid. I wanted blood. Her blood. That girl knew about me and Jeffrey. Of course, she didn't know all the intricate details, but Friend, that bitch knew he was off limits. Hell, everybody in my circle knew that. I don't care if we weren't talking. They all knew how much I loved him and definitely knew how much he loved me. Joy was there the night we had our last night of freedom get together. We talked about everything that night, and Jeffrey was one of those things. That bitch even saw the damn tears I shed that night about him. What the hell?

"Nyla. I am so sorry. You didn't want me and you made that very clear, but I promise you that I didn't know that was your friend. I never stopped thinking about you. I am always thinking about you. She made things easier because she seemed to know exactly what I liked and needed at the times I needed them."

"Of course the bitch knew. I fucking told her. All three of my girls know how I feel about you Jeffrey. That slimy slimy witch. She has broken the code."

"Nyla. I still and will always love you. I know you were meant to be mine. I know that. I know that."

"Jeffrey. You will not proclaim your love for me outside of this fucking Waffle House- especially after telling me that you've been fucking one of my friends, unknowingly or not. I really don't want to hear that right now."

"I know, Nyla I know, but I need you to know that I love you. I have only loved you."

"Bye, Jeffrey. I have something to do."

"Please Nyla."

"Jeffrey. I need some time. See you later."

"Okay, Nyla Baby."

I allowed him to hug me, and tried my best not to kiss him back when his lips touched mine. It took everything in me not to get in his passenger seat and drive away with the love of my life.

No, I couldn't be distracted. I had a slimy bitch ass friend to deal with in the Waffle House. This bitch! As I walked towards the door, I could see through the window that Joy wasn't at the table.

"Where is she?" I asked obviously annoyed.

"Who, Joy?" Sharon asked. I looked at her annoyed. "She's in the restroom. Why what happened?"

Without answering, I headed for the restroom door.

As I reached for the handle, she pulled and that was all I needed. I jumped on that double crossing back stabbing bitch like a wild rabbit dog. All you heard were screams from the bathroom.

By the time Sharon and Kendra reached the bathroom door and came in to break it up, it was too late. That bitch's blood was all over the place, and she fucking deserve it.

Every blow, every head to the mirror punch, and every kick to her body, everybody shot- she deserved it. She deserved them all and more.

All the shit we had been through- especially this semester, why would you ever cross me? I screamed as I delivered another Mike Tyson blow. I would have bit that bitch if they wouldn't have grabbed me, and like that I was up off the floor being carried out.

"Remember this ass whooping bitch the next time you ever think about crossing a bitch like me," is all I kept screaming as three unknown patrons carried me out of the bathroom and out of the Waffle house doors.

Kendra ran outside to the car, had me in it, and was driving off in 90 seconds flat.

"Kendra, take me to that bitch's house. Take me there now and where is Sharon?" I yelled.

Kendra just kept driving until far away enough to stop. As she slammed on breaks in the parking lot of Tallahassee Community College, she screamed, "What the hell is wrong with you Nyla? What in the hell was that about?"

She looked pissed and disappointed in me all at the same time and that made me even madder.

"Kendra, please. Do you even know what happened? Don't fucking scream at me girl."

"Nyla. I know you just damn near beat the life out of one of your friends and for what?"

"Kendra, the bitch has been fucking Jeffrey for the past month or so. She has been dating Jeffrey behind my back. I let that bitch into my heart and she betrayed me. She deserves to die, and I can make it happen."

Kendra just sat there in shock. Mouth wide open and then she started crying. That is all it took because there we were in the middle of a completely dark and empty TCC parking lot crying.

"Joy was like a sister to me." I promise every time I see her, I am going to whoop her ass, so she better leave Tallahassee if she knows what is best for her."

"Nyla. I'm sorry. That is really messed up for real. What kind of friend would ever do something like that? She is slimy, but Nyla you have got to calm down. I am thinking about your future right now because I know you are not and that is not good."

"Kendra, all I want is to beat the life out of her. She has messed with the wrong bitch. Don't she know where I am from and what I am capable of doing to her?"

"No, Nyla. I don't think she had any idea. If she did, she would not have even thought about doing this to you."

"Ken. Take me to Jeffrey's place please."

"What? Why?"

"Don't look at me like that. I'm not going to do anything crazy. I just want to talk to him."

"Okay, Nyla. I'll take you over there, but please don't get us locked up tonight."

"Ken. Have some faith in me please. I am not going to do anything that would get us arrested."

The closer we got to his house the more emotional I became. I didn't understand or know why. I knew I was still in love with him, but I didn't want to be with him anymore. I just wanted to know why he didn't want me. Why we could not be together but he would date Joy? I didn't understand it and I needed some answers. As we pulled up to his place, we waited patiently for someone to enter or exit the gate so we could go in. I didn't want him to know I was coming. After about ten minutes, someone finally decided to come home and in we went. As we turned the last corner onto his street, my heart was palpitating so hard. It felt like it was going to come out of my chest.

"Ken. I'll be back."

As I walked closer to his door, my hands began to shake. Everything began to shake.

I walked around the corner to his townhouse door entrance and stood there for a moment to get my nerves under control. I knocked on his door and began to rehearse my words in my head. I knocked again and didn't get an answer. I stood there for what seemed like hours, and as I turned to walk away, I heard a rustling in the trees behind me.

"Why are you here?" she screamed. Why are you here?"

I screamed in terror to see that she had a weapon.

"Jessie. Wait. Wait what are you doing?

"Answer my damn question. Why are you here?" she said almost foaming out of the mouth.

"I am here to talk to Jeffrey."

"Why? Why? You dumped him. Did you forget that?"

"Jessie, Jeffrey and I were never together. Please calm
down, and please stop pointing the gun at me."

"Why won't you just go away? Why? He would be
mine if you would just stay the hell away."

"Jessie, please."

At that moment and from the same direction in
which she came, someone slipped up behind Jessie as she
was lowering the gun and overpowered her.

She screamed uncontrollably and hit the ground.

One of the neighbors happened to see her out of his
window and came to help. He said he called the police, but
she looked like she was going to shoot me. Honestly, I
believe she would have killed me that night. Jessie had
become a fucking stalker and I think she had it in her to
pull the trigger.

Everywhere I went, it seemed like she was there.
Most of the times she would be alone and I wouldn't see
her until I was leaving the place. She would show up on
campus at random times when she should be in school over
two hundred miles away, but she seemed to always be in
Tallahassee. Some days, I would have like fifty missed
calls on my Caller Id from private numbers or random
numbers that I didn't recognize at all. She was a freakin nut
case. I would text Jeffrey and tell him to talk to her, but he

never took it seriously. He always tried to use me reaching out as a way to get back in good with me, and when I wouldn't respond he would get upset. I wish he had taken it more seriously. It was obvious that she wasn't just stalking me. Hell, her crazy ass was outside of his place with a gun.

As the neighbor overtook Jessie, the police pulled up and Kendra came running around the corner as well.

"What the hell happened here?" Kendra ran to me screaming in terror.

"Death almost happened here, Ken. Death."

Then of course, out of nowhere here he comes- the man of the hour, Jeffrey, pulling up to this near death scene. He just stared in disbelief as he realized these were people he knew. His steps became a bit swifter and more intentional as he saw me standing there. He continued to look puzzled as the police drove away with Jessie in the back seat looking like she wanted to snatch my heart out of my chest with her bare hands.

"Nyla, what happened?" He looked at us with confusion, fear and disbelief.

Ken was tired of the entire ordeal and she made it known.

"You, Jeffrey. You are what happened."

Continuing to look puzzled and with his mouth so wide open that he could capture a swarm of flies, he just shook his head as he continued to beg for answers.

Ken continued, "Nyla was almost arrested at the Waffle House because of you and shot to death in front of this apartment, your apartment, because of you. What the hell are you doing here? Why do you think it is okay to play these games and have these women going crazy over you?"

"Umm Kendra, with all due respect, I don't know what you are talking about? I love your friend. I am completely in love with her, but she doesn't want me. She didn't want me, our baby, our relationship- nothing. I love her. I have never loved someone the way I love her, and she doesn't want me. What am I supposed to do? I have tried calling and texting and emailing and sending letters to Nyla; she doesn't want me. She doesn't respond to any of my attempts to talk to her."

"Well tonight you almost lost every chance to ever say anything to her again! Jessie tried to kill her, asshole!"

"Wait! What the hell are you talking about Jeffrey? I have not received anything from you via mail and or electronically for that matter. Since I told you I was having the procedure done I have not heard from you. What are you talking about?"

"Nyla don't play dumb with me. Look," as he showed her message after message and email after email. I never received any of them.

I looked at him puzzled and in dismay.

What the hell happened to all the stuff Jeffrey sent to me, I thought. *That would be the next mystery to solve, after I figure out this situation in front of me.*

I wasn't going to let him know that I was softening up, so I looked at him with fury in my eyes. "We need to talk Jeffrey."

As Ken started walking towards his place too, I said, "Ken, since he is home now can you give me a few minutes?"

"No!" She looked back and forth between the two of us. "Hell no, as a matter of fact."

"Kendra, if you don't mind, I will bring her home as soon as we are done talking." Jeffery spoke in his calmest tone to try and ease Ken's peace of mind.

"Oh, I guess you all didn't hear me huh?" She tried to match his calm tone of voice, but her efforts were not successful.

"Hell no you won't be bringing her home after your talk because I am not leaving her here with you." Kendra's voice was raising syllable by syllable.

"Who knows what other bitches might jump off the roof or break down your door to get your attention? No sir, my friend has had enough surprises for the night. I will be waiting right in your living room on the couch. Yup, lead the way Alfred; lead the fuckin' way."

I chuckled and just followed because I knew my friend, and she wasn't leaving.

As Jeffrey led the way back down the sidewalk, which led to his front door, Kendra surveyed our surroundings. She surveyed the damn area like she was working for the secret service.

"Ken, it is okay," I said watching her look around like a guard dog in attack mode.

"No, hell. It's not okay. I'll be damned if another one of his tricks jumps out of some bushes again on you."

Jeffrey knew he was fighting a losing battle, so he didn't even try to convince Kendra that he wasn't seeing anyone. He knew that she wouldn't believe anything he said. Hell I barely believed anything he said these days.

He opened the door to his place I had grown to love so much. This was Kendra's first time in his place and though she tried not to show that she was impressed with his house, she was and actually had to tell him.

"Nice place," she grumbled at him.

"Thank you." He made no eye contact.

"Kendra you can make yourself at home. Do you mind if Nyla and I talk in here? He pointed to the game room and I objected.

"No, we can't talk in there."

Kendra looked puzzled but knew that must have been the place where all the magic happened.

"I'll go in there and you all can sit right here where there is plenty of light."

Jeffrey just looked at both of us defeated and Kendra proceeded to walk ever so slowly to the game room.

His eyes never left mine and as soon as he heard the door close behind Kendra, he began to speak. But before he could, I slapped the shit out of him. I mean an Angela Bassett and Ike Turner slap. I wanted him to feel my pain and since he couldn't feel it internally he could at least feel it externally.

He just looked at me as if he deserved it and didn't even try to defend himself. Hell, he didn't even try to put his hands up to block another blow if another one was coming. I suppose he knew there wasn't another one, and he was right.

I only had that one for him. I'm not a violent woman. I was just hurt and had been holding that inside for a while.

"You just keep hurting me. Why do you keep hurting me?" And there we were in the middle of his living room crying. I just slid to the floor and he wouldn't let me fall. He scooped me up and carried me to the couch and just let me sob.

He was always good like that. He knew what to do and when to do it. We cried in each other's arms for what seemed like forever; he just let my tears soak his shirt like a wet t-shirt contest and never said a word.

"Jeffrey why do you keep hurting me?"

"Nyla that is not what I ever wanted to do. You won't let me love you. You don't want to be with me, and I can't stand the thought of you being with anyone else. Shit, I can't stand the thought of being with anyone else."

"So why Joy?"

"To pass the time. To try and get over you and no matter what she might have told you we never even had a deep kiss let alone sex. I couldn't do it. I haven't been with anyone else since you."

I felt like I shouldn't believe him but I did. I did believe him. I believed anything he told me and that could have been his biggest strength with me. I believed in him, and at that moment I just stared at him. I couldn't say a word. As he stared into my eyes and kissed me, I didn't resist him.

I let him kiss me over and over again because as much as he missed me, I missed him too, and even though he hadn't been with anyone else, I had. But that wasn't his business to know. I just closed my eyes and continued to let him heal me with his kisses.

Chapter 44- Reality Hits

As I opened my eyes that next morning, tears streamed down my face. It felt so real, and I wanted it to be true, but it was just a dream. Jeffrey didn't come home and after the police left with Jessi in handcuffs, we left. It made me even madder because as we walked to the car I kept thinking, *where the fuck is he?*

299

Then I said it out loud- "Ken, where the fuck was he? Why hasn't he called me? Why isn't he here?" She had spent the night.

She just looked at me, lost for words.

Sharon was not home; she was probably still with her bitch ass hoe of a line sister doctoring her wounds, but I didn't give a shit. I hope that slut feels my wrath for weeks, and I dare her ass to try and press charges. I just dare her.

All of a sudden, a sea of emotions overtook me, and I found myself on the floor. I mean, Friend I was spread out just resting in the solitude of the hardwood floors that made my tears form into a puddle that seemed to me like a sea. I just cried and cried and cried. I felt like shit rolled over twice, and as I laid there, I could see it, my sister's diary glowing like she was drawing me to her. I knew that Ty and I said we would read it together, but he would forgive me for doing this without him once he heard about the shit show of a night I had just lived through.

I opened it and immediately began to cry. This was my sister's handwriting. These were her words.

Dear Diary,

I've decided today is the day. I have tried to be my best and I'm tired. I'm tainted and broken. I am responsible

300

for it all. They can't tell me different because I know I am. I have always loved my uncle and in ways I shouldn't have and now he's gone. He's gone. I got him killed and all I want is to be with him. My uncle was my first and nobody would ever understand it. We tried to be so careful, but it didn't work and now he's dead. He was only 7 years older than me and he wasn't even my blood. Grandma and Grandpa saved him from hell. They were always doing stuff like that. He was their neighbor's grandbaby, and his mother and father were on drugs. He was being abused and they saved him just like he saved me, but now he is dead.

When my mother killed my baby brother, I was destroyed. I was traumatized and scared and angry and depressed. My uncle was the only one that understood, and that felt good. He was my first true love Diary. We would just talk and talk and talk for hours. I know everyone thought I had a boyfriend, and I did- it was him. We didn't plan for any of it to happen. No one would understand and we didn't know how to tell anyone. That night when he was caught leaving my room- oh my God Diary, why? Why did it have to be this way? No one let him explain. No one let me explain and now he is dead and I want to die, too. I am going to be with him and my baby brother. Everyone will be okay- even when I am gone. Nyla has Ty, and they'll be fine.

I just sobbed and sobbed and sobbed. Ken didn't interrupt- she knew how heartbreak sounded, but then there was a knock on my door that interrupted my tears and I was relieved. I ran out of my room past Ken who was slowly rising to answer it. I was thinking it was Ty or Sharon, and I could fall into their arms.

I opened the door to his beautiful face and just fell into his chest.

"Nyla, I love you. I have been driving around for hours trying to get the nerve to come here. I'm so sorry."

I just talked to him through his chest. "It took you long enough. I love you too."

www.ingramcontent.com/pod-product-compliance
Lightning Source LLC
Chambersburg PA
CBHW020945260626
47169CB00006B/1834